AN ARTFUL DECEIT

HOLLY NEWMAN

Created with Vellum

CHAPTER 1
THE SKETCH

The Viscount Sebastian Redinger's blond Adonis good looks were marred by more than bruises and bandages. A petulant frown pulled at his features when he saw his butler at the door of his bedchamber with a visiting card on a silver salver.

"Who is it now, Randolph? If it's Timmy Wainbottom or Jerry Jessup or Chester Harley come to gloat, tell them I'm napping, or some such thing. I'll not abide their snickers. It was all their fault. I just went along for the giggles." He plucked restlessly at his bedcovers.

"I'm sure it is as you say, my lord, but it is neither of those two gentlemen. If it had been, I assure you I would have sent them roundly about their business," his butler said crisply.

Redinger grinned, quite in his old manner. "You're a right one, you are, and no mistake. It was my fortunate day when I stole you from my parents' employ."

"Thank you, my lord," Randolph solemnly returned, not a muscle in his cheek twitching to betray that the Earl of Galborough was paying him a handsome fee to watch out for his errant heir. And that in addition to his wages from Redinger.

Randolph wondered what the old earl would say to this latest escapade. Done himself up good, the young master had. Nonetheless, he consoled himself against his employers' anger with the knowledge that he had hitherto managed to steer their heir clear from the clutches of a certain breed of females. And it looked like Redinger was about to take the plunge into precisely the sort of marriage his esteemable parents desired. If it came to pass, Randolph was sure his retirement would be in refined comfort. The Earl and Countess of Galborough were most generous for what they considered onerous labor. But this was not for the Viscount's knowledge, and his duty still demanded he act as Redinger's man.

"If I may be so bold, my lord, I venture to say this guest shall be a welcome respite from your pain." He handed Redinger the card. "The Duke of Ellinbourne is below."

"Miles Wingate? Here? In the city? Why I say, that is fabulous news!" The Viscount stared at the card a moment, grinning broadly. He waved peremptorily at his man. "Well, don't just stand there like a clodhead, Randolph, show him up! Show him up!"

Randolph bowed. "Immediately, my lord."

A moment later, Randolph opened the door to the bedchamber to admit Miles Wingate, Sixth Duke of Ellinbourne. The Duke paused on the threshold, a rare smile cracking his habitually reserved countenance as he took in his cousin's battered appearance as he lay amid a pile of lace-edged white pillows and cut red velvet bedcovers and hangings. The late morning sun streaming across the bed back-lit his blond hair—now in wild disarray—like a halo. Miles's fingers drummed the sketchbook he held, composition ideas immediately forming in his mind.

Redinger grimaced back at him. "Come in, come in. I know, don't say it. I've come a cropper." With a sweeping motion, his good arm indicated his bandaged and bruised face, and his arm trussed up in a black silk sling.

Miles nodded wryly at Redinger's understatement. He walked into the room and murmured his thanks as he sat down in the chair Randolph drew up for him by the bed. He returned his attention to his cousin, his brown eyes closely examining Redinger's face in the bright sunlight cast on it through the open window curtains, his lips twitching against laughter. "I must say that is the most interesting shade of purple, mottled with yellow and green on the side of your face. I wonder if I could reproduce it with paints?"

"Humph." Redinger turned his head away from the glaring light, then his lips reluctantly twisted into a smile. His eyes slid toward Miles, ruefully conceding his right to amusement.

"Might make an interesting portrait. Think the earl would mount it along the stairway with the others?" Miles mused.

Redinger guffawed, then gasped, clutching his side. He shook his head, then gulped as the sharp stabbing pain caused by his laughter subsided and he found his voice. "No room, thank God! And knowing him, he would. Object lesson and all that rubbish. Then again, you being a Duke and all now, he wouldn't approve."

"Ah, yes, let me see . . ." Miles laid one long finger alongside his nose. "He'd deem it not quite proper and a bit too plebeian?"

"That's it."

The Duke leaned back in the chair and stretched out his legs. "I was an artist long before I became a duke."

"Everyone knows that. Just that my father thinks you should put that behind you."

"I know, but almost until it happened, within days even, I had no expectations of the title. Or its responsibilities." Miles said, exasperation eloquent in his voice. He ran a hand through his wavy brown hair. "I'd be a hypocrite to my art if I let a title change all that— to say nothing of the insult to those who went before me. I've had enough changes in my life," he finished softly, a hint of bitterness in his voice.

Redinger nodded sympathetically. He knew his cousin's history only too well, for Miles Wingate's father's living had been in the Earl of Galborough's gift. To rise from the younger son of a country parson to Duke of Ellinbourne had not been a smooth transition for Miles. It was an elevation he still grappled with. For a time, he'd even contemplated the almost unheard of, repudiating the title. That he hadn't spoke volumes for Miles' sense of honor and duty. Redinger knew he would have been hard-pressed to follow his cousin's example. Then again, that could be considered a given, for no two men seemed less likely to form a firm friendship—even as cousins. Redinger was flighty and up for all manner of pranks and fun. He lived comfortably in society, reveling in its glitter and gaiety. Miles preferred quiet, his nature more serious. He preferred hours before his easel with paint pots and brushes to hours in the ballrooms or society's clubs.

"But what brings you to the city?" Redinger asked, never one to dwell on dismal matters. "Thought you were fixed forever on that estate of yours."

Miles quite willingly accepted his change of subject. "The Royal Academy of Arts is due to open again in a couple of weeks, and I have a picture accepted for the next showing."

"No! You don't say! By Jove, that's jolly good news!"

"I think so. There was some question as to my eligibility—now. Your father is not alone in his opinion. Dukes patronize art; they don't create it."

Redinger waved his hand dismissively. "These are modern times. People have to learn to adjust."

Miles laughed. "And is it these 'modern times' that make boxing the watch acceptable?"

Redinger had the grace to look discomfited. "You heard about that."

"Almost upon rising. Of course, the thrust of the story was how comical you looked, trapped underneath the watchman's box with the poor fellow still inside cursing you all."

"Yes, well, it weren't so comical to feel. And Wainbottom, Jessup, and Harley just stood there and laughed. I've half a mind to call 'em out when I recover. It was their idea. And their fault it fell on me! And that watchman weren't no poor fellow."

"Not according to their story."

"Whatever it is, they're lying. I was in a muddle with a devil of a head, and here's this gent calling out all's well when I knew my head hurt too much for it to be well. And so I said to Wainbottom. He giggled, as he does, and told me to tell that to the old man myself. So I come up to the box and try to tell him this, you see, but he's not listening. Dry old stick. So I jump up to hang onto the side and to get closer. That's when Wainbottom's giggles get the best of him and Jessup joins in and both lean against the box from the opposite side, too helpless to stand up.

The old man's shout'n at us and batt'n me with his cane. I didn't care none for this so I grabbed it. That's when the box started to tumble toward me. I landed on my back in the mud. Ruined my best jacket, it did."

"To say nothing of your arm, side, or face."

"Oh, the face weren't from the fall. That was from that damned old gent's cudgel. Caught me good, he did. I'd like to cudgel him, I tell you. At least Timmy, Jerry, and Chester had the decency to get me out of there then. Wouldn't do to be found on one's back in the dirt, you know."

Miles muffled a laugh at Redinger's sincere tone. "No, I don't suppose it would."

"Don't laugh. 'Tis the truth."

Miles straightened and adopted his most noncommittal expression. "To be sure. But who's laughing?"

"Well, it looked suspiciously like you were."

"Me? Oh, come now, Sebastian, I'm much too sober a fellow, or so you've always told me."

"So you are! Most of the time. Leastwise with other people. But I remember—"

"Excuse me, my lord. May I offer you gentlemen refreshments?" Redinger's butler asked from the bedchamber doorway, a silver tray in hand bearing drinks, tea for the invalid and Madeira for his guest.

"Capital idea, Randolph," Redinger said with relief. "But what's this? Tea? Oh, wipe that mutinous expression from your face, I dashed well remember what that quack doctor said. All right, I'll drink it. But see if Mrs. Mendall has any of those cakes of hers that I like so well. Poppyseed with icing. Simply smashing," he told Miles as Randolph bowed and left the room. "See if you don't agree."

Redinger subsided and was silent, a deep crease

incised on his brow. He plucked at his bedcovers, his eyes not meeting his cousin's.

Miles cocked his head and raised his eyebrows.

"You can't know how dashed glad I am to see you, Miles. This," he waved at his injuries, "has come at a devilishly awkward time."

"Really?" Miles prompted. He studied his cousin. It wasn't like Redinger to be so cut up over anything. Almost absentmindedly, he flipped open his sketchbook and pulled a piece of charcoal wrapped in paper from his pocket.

"Mother and father have been after me to get married and produce an heir." He gave a bark of laughter. "They're afraid my ramshackle existence will lead to an early grave, and if the next in line ain't accounted for by me, the title will go to some plebeian nobody cousin."

"As the Ellinbourne title did," the Duke said drily as he quickly sketched the battered and brooding image of the Viscount.

Redinger flushed. "Didn't mean it like that. And dash it all, Miles, that ain't fair. They never thought you a nobody. As if anyone could! It was just that, well, just that...."

Miles looked up from his drawing. "That being an artist is beneath thought."

Redinger shrugged and shifted uncomfortably beneath his cousin's steady regard.

Miles sighed and relented. "So, they desire you to marry. Do they have your bride chosen?"

"Yes. Been chosen nearly since she was born. The dearest wish of my grandmother and hers, and all that."

"So much for your modern times."

"Well, I don't object. I would if I could find my

Juliet, but I lost her a year ago. It was the damnedest thing, too. I could have sworn she loved me, and I her. But one day she just wasn't there anymore."

"And so heartbroken, you're bravely going to forget her and marry another."

"This ain't a jest. I've got my duty, and frankly, I just don't care."

The Duke frowned. "That doesn't seem fair to your chosen bride, does it?"

Redinger glanced away. "From what I remember of her, Miss Hallowell always was a good sort." He looked back at the Duke. "Surely you met her. Came to the estate once with her parents. Or was that when you were away?"

"I'm sure I don't know and can't tell you until you tell me the identity of this fortunate young woman destined to be Viscountess Redinger and then Countess of Galborough."

"Oh, yes. Well, 'tis Miss Hallowell. Miss Ann Hallowell. Father was Graham Hallowell. Died two years back."

Miles shook his head. "Haven't heard of them."

"Heard of her grandmother, though, I'll venture. The Dowager Countess of Malmsby."

Miles paused and whistled softly, then he laughed. "That is a name I've heard. How could I not? Hers is a name well known in art circles. Her private collection of art at Versely Park is rumored to be outstanding. Perhaps the best in the nation. If not the best, then certainly the largest! But nobody outside her family has seen it in over five years."

Redinger nodded. "Until now. She's having a house party beginning Friday."

Miles's light brown eyebrows rose.

"I was to attend and while there solicit Miss Hallowell's hand in marriage. It's been all arranged."

"But now—"

"It's obvious I cain't go. Couldn't take the jostling in a carriage to get there, or on a horse for that matter. That's what that cursed bonesetter said. Wouldn't want to go anyway with a phizz like this."

"Yes, it does spoil the pretty boy image."

Redinger grimaced at his cousin. "Been trying to come up with a way to send my regrets gracefully. Party set up particularly so I could pop the question. Deuced awkward."

"Yes, I see what you mean."

"I've been turning it over and over in my mind, how I'm going to write and tell them I cain't go. Are those the cakes, Randolph? Well, don't just stand there, man, bring them in! Now, what was I saying? Oh, yes, the worst is I still have to tell my parents. They're invited, too, naturally."

"Begging your pardon, my lord," Randolph interrupted as he set the dish of cakes on the table by the bed, "but while the doctor was with you, I took the liberty of sending a letter to inform the Earl and Countess of your unfortunate accident."

"You did? Why? No, never mind. I'd not a mind to write that note anyway."

"As you say, my lord."

"But that still leaves the Hallowells to tell, and I'd hate just to send round a note."

"Why not?" Miles asked while eying askance the cake with an excessive amount of sugary icing. He hoped Redinger would not press him to sample this treat.

Redinger grabbed the largest piece of cake from the plate. "I remember Miss Hallowell as a shy little thing. Wouldn't want to hurt her." He took a bite of the cake. "Countin' on me, ya know," he mumbled, his mouth full.

Miles took a sip of his Madeira, then returned the nearly full glass to the table at his elbow and resumed sketching. "Is she that far past her prayers?"

"What?" Redinger swallowed and cleared his throat. "Oh, no. No, not that at all. Miss Hallowell ain't long in the tooth, if that's what you're asking. Her stepmother and my mother been corresponding. They set the whole up between them. No, the thing is, it seems a shabby trick to send round a note." He took another bite, his expression eloquent of satisfaction with the cake.

"It doesn't appear as if it can be helped," Miles said.

Redinger shook his head in contradiction, then cleared his throat again. "Yes, it can! You could step around to their house and tell them for me."

"Me?"

"Not quite so bad coming from a duke and all."

Miles grimaced.

"Won't be that bad. I'll give you a letter to deliver to Mrs. Hallowell and a poem for Miss Hallowell."

"A poem!" Miles and Randolph said at once.

Miles looked at the butler in surprise. He suddenly realized he had been standing at the side of the room, unabashedly listening to their conversation. The man was too forward for his taste.

"Yes, certainly, a poem," repeated Redinger, warming to the idea. He looked from Miles to his butler and back. "It's all the crack, poetry is. Women love it. Taken to writing it myself, haven't I, Randolph?"

"You?"

Redinger nodded, his eyes alight with pleasure. "I'm not bad, either. Composing a poem about the accident. Just a little ditty. It's not done yet. When it is, I'll send you round a copy. Got a poem for Miss Hallowell, too. Just the ticket. Wrote it for a pretty little opera dancer I was taken with. Randolph convinced me it were too good to waste on someone who most likely couldn't appreciate its fine qualities, didn't you, my man? Daresay Miss Hallowell will like it instead."

"But, my lord!" protested Randolph, a pained expression pulling his normally pinched face tighter.

Miles tried biting his lower lip to keep from laughing. It didn't work. Randolph's expression was too comical. It was apparent Redinger's glib explanation was far from the mark as far his butler was concerned.

"What's so funny about that?" Redinger asked in high dudgeon.

Miles choked back his laughter. "Sorry. Never pictured you as the poetic type."

"Well, if you wouldn't bury yourself in the country, you'd know you ain't the only clever fellow."

"I'm sorry for laughing. Truly. You took me by surprise. I'd no notion you'd become a man of such wide —ah—sensibilities."

Redinger allowed himself to be mollified, though he wasn't entirely sure as to his cousin's meaning.

"Randolph, get me that poem—it's the one I tied up with a purple ribbon. Yes, that's it." He held it for a moment in his hands, then thrust it into Miles's. "Here, take this to Miss Hallowell."

"Oh, but, my lord, I don't believe that one would be quite appropriate," protested the butler, his hand reaching for the scroll.

Redinger batted his hand away. "Hush, don't worry, Randolph. You're an old woman. Miss Hallowell is a woman of taste and refinement; she'll appreciate the poem. Now, bring me a writing desk so I can dash off a note to Mrs. Hallowell."

"Right away, my lord," acquiesced the defeated butler. He exchanged a pained, speaking look with the Duke.

The Duke shrugged, then took pity on the man. He looked back at the Viscount. "Sebastian," he said seriously, tapping the scroll against his sketchbook, "perhaps this isn't a good idea."

"Yes, it is. Much nicer than a note sent round by a servant. After all, you're a duke!"

"Not you, too!"

"Sorry. Are you finished with that thing yet?"

Miles glanced down at the sketchbook in his lap. "Yes, and I believe I've captured the true spirit of your injuries, as you would have them," he said with a smile.

Redinger reached for the sketchbook, wincing as he twisted toward Miles. "Damn sawbones has me wrapped too tight."

The Duke let him take the sketch from his lap, his brown eyes shining with mirth.

"What's this?" Redinger laughed then hastily stopped, clasping his hand to his side. The quick sketch portrayed Redinger leaning back against his nest of pillows, his expression below his bandaged brow one of sacrificial suffering.

"It's the tragically wounded hero who remains noble in his suffering. It matches your poetic ideal."

Redinger laughed again then begged Miles not to make him laugh for it hurt too much. "But it is a devil-ishly clever sketch. Damned clever. Strap me if that don't give me an idea! Take that picture to Miss Hallowell along with the poem. More believable. Prove I'm not trying to give her the slip."

"Would she think that?"

Redinger shrugged. "Women are funny creatures. But you mark my words, she'll be vastly entertained with the poem and sketch." He nodded sagely. "Vastly," he repeated, feeling smug.

The sixth Duke of Ellinbourne leaned back in his chair as he wondered just what it was he'd gotten himself into. He reached for his Madeira glass, this time downing its contents with a single swallow. Something told him he should have stayed on his estate in the country.

CHAPTER 2

THE DRESS

"Eikes!"

Ann Hallowell whirled around to see what had her stepmother screeching like a mouse had run over her toes. To her consternation, Ursula Hallowell had picked up her gray-colored day dress from where Ann had laid it across her bed for her maid, Lucy, to pack. She gingerly held the dress up by her fingertips as if it actually were a revolting mouse.

"I like that dress. It's comfortable," Ann said as she came away from her armoire, another load of linens in her arms.

"Comfortable!" Ursula exclaimed, staring at Ann in disbelief. "What has comfort to do with fashion? This—this rag was barely suitable for half-mourning! It is, perhaps, more in keeping for a governess or companion, but for you?" She clucked her tongue and shook her head, sending a profusion of blond curls bouncing. "No, and no, and no!"

"I like to wear that dress when I'm sketching outdoors," Ann explained as she kneeled next to the large traveling trunk the footman had placed in the middle of her bedroom.

Ursula shuddered. "A fine thing it would be for the future Countess of Galborough to be seen traipsing about Versely Park looking like a servant! And what they would say of me? I'd be called the wicked stepmother."

Ann laughed. "You? Wicked? Now you are doing it too brown."

"No, I am not. You have no notion how society tongues wag!" Ursula said, her voice trembling.

"Oh, Ursula," Ann said as she sat back on her heels. Ursula had suffered many an unkind comment about her marriage to Graham Hallowell, a gentleman with a daughter nearly her age.

"Well, I'm certainly glad I decided to oversee your packing," Ursula said, rallying. She looked down at the dress she still held. "Praise be that your maid is belowstairs ironing your dark blue gown. That I will accept. It will be suitable for wearing while sketching out of doors. But not this! Nor for a future countess!"

Ursula Hallowell wadded up the offending gray dress and threw it into a corner of Ann's bedroom.

Ann bit her lower lip against a sharp retort as she stared at the crumpled heap. Finally, she sighed and shook her head. "Ursula, nothing is settled, yet," she said, infusing her voice with a calmness she far from felt. "You and the Countess of Galborough may have hatched a notion between you that Redinger and I should wed; but ultimately that decision will be between the Viscount and me."

"It is not our notion," Ursula feebly protested, "though we concur it is an eminently suitable match. It was, after all, the dearest wish of your grandmother and the dear departed Dowager Countess of Galborough."

Ann inelegantly snorted. "It was just grandmotherly musings on both sides. The late Dowager Countess of Galborough would be the first to argue against this absurd notion for her grandson," she said, ignoring her stepmother's condemning frown as she placed her linens in the bottom of the leather-bound trunk.

Ursula disagreed. "We don't know that; and besides, your grandmother, the Dowager Duchess of Malmsby, has not said anything against the match. She's been most amenable to it." She sat down on the edge of Ann's bed, her expression determined.

Ann stood up and placed her hands on her hips. "And most likely grandmother wouldn't object, not if she remembers what I look like. I am not marriageable. It is the Galboroughs who are likely to run when they discover my disfigurement."

Ann's body seemed to collapse in upon herself on hearing her words. She kneeled on the floor by the bed, grabbing Ursula's hands in hers. "Oh Ursula, this was an insane idea! A cruel idea! How could you do this to me?"

Ursula softly smiled as she shook her head. "You talk nonsense, my dear. Your scars are larger in your eyes than in any others." She gently pulled on Ann's arms to get her to stand up again. "Truthfully, that scar on your face is scarcely noticeable, and you know you only limp when you overexert yourself," Ursula reminded her.

Ann laughed hollowly as she sat down on the bed next to Ursula and put her arms around her stepmother's slender shoulders. "Yours, bless your heart, are loving eyes blinded to the truth. No. Do not argue," she said, as she felt Ursula stiffen. "I promised I would meet with Viscount Redinger, and so I shall. But I'll

not have coercion from either side. Do you understand me?"

Ursula Hallowell pouted prettily. "I'm hurt that
you don't trust me. I have your best interests at heart,
after all, I am your mother."

Ann Hallowell laughed again, this time the sound
bubbling up freely, rippling through her. She fell
backward on the bed, struggling to catch her breath
between giggles.

"Mother? Ursula!" Ann gasped out, her eyes watering. She lifted her head from the peach-colored counterpane. "If you could only see yourself! It is so
ludicrous! It always has been! You are a head shorter
than I am, petite and delicate compared to my gimpy
long-legged Meg figure. And though seven years separate us in age, I swear you have ever looked the
younger and doubtlessly will ever do so!"

Ann struggled up onto her elbows. "Truth be told,
I have been more your companion and mentor than
stepdaughter these last two years since father died.
And I understand," she said conspiratorially, "about
Colonel Brantley."

Ursula stiffened. "Honestly, Ann, I don't know
what you are babbling about. What about Colonel
Brantley? There is nothing to understand. We are
merely good friends, for he is a delightful escort."

"Of course," Ann drawled, vastly amused by the
high color suddenly blooming on Ursula's fair cheeks.

A knock at the door sobered Ann. She sat up. "Yes,
what is it?"

Isley, the Hallowell butler for as long as Ann could
remember, opened the door. "Pardon madam, . . . miss,
but the Duke of Ellinbourne is below."

"The Duke of Ellinbourne!" Ursula exclaimed,
rising to her feet.

"Yes, madam. Shall I tell the Duke you shall be down directly?"

Ursula ignored the butler's question. She hurried toward the dressing table mirror to check her hair.

"Who's he?" Ann asked. "The name's familiar, but I cannot think why."

"Honestly, my dear, you never pay attention to gossip. Just last evening Lady Jersey was speaking of him. Were you not attending?" Ursula straightened her lace cap, tucking a wayward blond curl back into place.

"No. I attend to her as little as possible." Ann scowled. "The woman is a menace. I don't know how you can like her."

"Madam—" Isley said.

"I don't," Ursula confessed, turning away from the mirror. "But she is one of Almacks' most influential patronesses, and she knows everyone and everything. One must keep abreast of society."

Ann shrugged. "So you say. Frankly, the whole bores me," she said with contrived lightness.

It was only in the small recesses of her mind that she admitted society scared her. In the five years since that Boxing Day hunt when she'd injured herself, she'd come to accept her physical limitations. What she couldn't conquer was society's whispered comments and pitying stares. In reaction, she shunned society as best she might.

Ursula waved her hand dismissively. "Ennui is fashionable."

"Madam," Isley said again, louder.

Ursula turned to look at the butler. She frowned. "What? Oh, yes. Direct His Grace to the blue salon and tell him we shall be down directly."

"Yes, madam. Thank you, madam," Isley said with a sigh and a bow.

"We?" Ann protested. "No thank you,"

Overhearing her protest, Isley turned back toward the room. "I beg your pardon, miss, but His Grace did ask to see both of you. He said something about a message from the Viscount Redinger." He bowed again, apologetically, and left to descend the stairs.

Ann rose from the bed. "Oh, fie! Worse and worse!" she exclaimed, theatrically clinging to a bedpost. "Redinger is already reneging." She grinned and leaned back against the post. "Just as well. Perhaps now I shall be able to enjoy my visit with grandmother, study her art collection at leisure, and do some outdoor sketching."

"Ellinbourne and Redinger," murmured Ursula. "I had no notion they were acquainted." She stared pensively at the bedroom door to the hall as if she could see through it and down to their visitor below. "If I'd known I would have been sure to have his name included on this house party list. Bother. The numbers will be uneven if we include another male at this date." She turned back to look at Ann. "Can you think of another single female, preferably elderly, whom we could hurriedly invite?"

"Poor Brantley!" Ann said.

"You think . . . ." Ursula began, astonishment clear on her face.

"Perhaps you could un-invite Colonel Brantley," Ann suggested. "It might be kinder than allowing him to suffer while you cast your lures for the Duke."

Ursula laughed and shook her head. "You are far off the mark. But since you do not know of Ellinbourne, I suppose that is to be expected. Come, straighten your fichu, and let's meet our guest. It is not socially politic to leave a duke kicking his heels."

"Oh, I don't know. That sounds like an apropos occupation for most."

Ursula clucked her tongue and pushed Ann's slow-moving hands out of the way so she could arrange the ivory lace fichu at the top of Ann's fawn-colored gown. She wrinkled her nose as she noted what dress Ann wore, but inwardly shrugged. At least it was not that horrid gray thing.

"Not your mother, eh?" Ursula teased as she stepped away and looked at Ann. She was not beautiful, not in the classical sense, but there was such elegance in her, especially when she smiled. And Ann really had no notion of it. Such a travesty.

Ursula tucked Ann's arm in hers and led her toward the door.

CHAPTER 3
THE GUEST

Miles studied the watercolor painting hanging over the small, French gilt writing desk set between the parlor windows that fronted the street. It was an amateur painting. The color opacity and the too symmetrical composition shouted amateur status. Nonetheless, the painting pleased the eye for the unknown artist possessed a nice sense of light and a clean color sense. Its simple, pastoral composition also stood in its favor.

Curious, he leaned over the desk to read the tiny, faint signature inscribed in the bottom right corner. The size and spideriness of the signature could indicate the unknown artist's dissatisfaction or embarrassment with their work.

He quickly identified Hallowell as the last name. He braced his knuckles against the gleaming desk surface as he peered closer. "Ann!" he triumphantly read aloud.

"I beg your pardon?"

Miles turned around. In the open parlor doorway stood two very different women. The shorter had the much-revered china doll prettiness of blond hair, blue eyes, and fair, unblemished skin. Her expression was one of open curiosity. A tiny smile curved her perfect bow-shaped pink lips upwards. If this was Miss Hallowell, they would account Redinger a fortunate fellow to capture this beautiful morsel. However, the other woman captured his interest.

Taller than most women, he judged her to be, perhaps, only four inches shorter than himself. Her marmalade-colored hair looked between butter and toast. She wore her hair severely pulled back, save for a few curls coaxed around her face in bare homage to the prevailing style. Her eyes were Mediterranean blue, clear, and direct beneath fair, well arched light-brown brows that lent her a perpetual 'surprised by life' look. Her skin glowed, attesting to long hours outdoors. Against the warm, tan glow a white, crescent-shaped scar on her chin stood out, but she didn't tuck her head down to minimize its effect as many women, and men, would have. She met the world with it straight on. Miles found himself fascinated.

"Mrs. Hallowell, please forgive this intrusion," he began, addressing the taller woman.

Ann's lips twitched. She looked down at Ursula. "See what I mean?"

Ursula Hallowell looked up at Ann and nodded wryly. Then she stepped forward. "Your Grace, I am Mrs. Hallowell," she said.

"Your pardon, madam," Miles said. He lifted her hand to bestow a chaste salute and felt a sharp twinge of disappointment.

Mrs. Hallowell shrugged prettily. "You are not the first. I doubt you shall be the last," she said with a laugh. She gestured toward Ann. "This is my step-daughter, Miss Ann Hallowell."

The Duke bowed. "I was just admiring your watercolor, Miss Hallowell. You have a nice sense of color and subject."

She glanced toward the painting, then laughed self-effacingly. "Ursula would insist on hanging it."

"I like it," Mrs. Hallowell said flatly. Then she smiled broadly at the Duke. "Please, won't you sit down, your grace?" She led him to a cozy seating arrangement by the fireplace. Miss Hallowell, he noted, trailed quietly behind her, though he thought he detected the hint of amusement in her eyes. His eyes narrowed in curiosity at her slow, stately, and slightly off-balanced gait. However, his attention was soon claimed by Mrs. Hallowell who smiled up at him, her manner flirtatious, but without, to his relief, any real interest.

Mrs. Hallowell motioned her butler, who'd followed them into the room, to serve sherry, and then she sat in one of the blue, silk-covered chairs closest to the white marble fireplace. "My butler said you have a message for us from the Viscount Redinger. I trust he is still planning on attending the house party?" she said as she gestured her invitation for him to take the seat opposite her.

"Regrettably, no," he replied as he flicked up the tails of his coat and settled in the matching blue silk-covered chair while Miss Hallowell sat on a nearby small, blue and gold striped sofa.

"What?!" Ursula demanded, half-rising to her feet, then self-consciously sitting down again. She glanced at Ann and Miles followed her lead. Miss Hallowell seemed to take amusement from his announcement, much to Mrs. Hallowell's consternation.

"Not but that he wishes to, however," Miles hastened to add, as he looked from one woman to the other, curious as to the sudden undercurrents in the room. "It is just that he has met with a slight accident."

"An accident! He is not dead, is he?" Mrs. Hallowell shrieked.

"No, no, calm yourself, madam. Nothing like that, I assure you. He's just, well . . ." Miles could feel warmth rise to his cheeks and felt like a bloody schoolboy. Silent, he cursed Redinger for tasking him with this duty and himself for agreeing. "Redinger will be laid up for a while."

"What happened?" Miss Hallowell asked, leaning forward slightly. She looked interested despite herself. Curious.

Miles stroked his chin with his knuckles. "I've always pondered what the correct response would be in these situations. I now realize there is none," he confessed, ruefully smiling. Though Mrs. Hallowell sat directly across from him, he found himself turning more and more to face Miss Hallowell.

Ann Hallowell laughed delightedly, enjoying the Duke's rueful smile, and everything else about the gentleman. His blue superfine coat faced in black showed a casual elegance. Only a single fob on a plain gold chain hung from his buff-colored waistcoat, which matched his buff-colored pantaloons. He lacked ostentation; but drew attention to himself with his calm, self-assured manner. His wavy, dusky–brown hair had escaped the pomade pot and fell forward across his wide brow. But most of all, it was his eyes that drew her attention, for they were the golden-brown color of the sherry Isley had poured into her glass.

"Ah, the quandary of the truth versus the social lie," she managed to say lightly.

"Exactly," he said, his warm sherry gaze holding hers.

Breathless, Ann deliberately broke eye contact. "Oh, well, let's have the truth. I'm sure it's much more interesting."

Faced with explaining Redinger's absence, Miles suddenly felt like a damn poacher. Ann Hallowell fascinated him as no woman had. And she was his cousin's intended. His jaw clenched as he leaned back in his chair. "That would depend on your point of view," he said more formally.

Miss Hallowell cocked her head as she considered that. "Yes, I suppose that would be true.

"Redinger is not amused."

She laughed again. "The victim seldom is. Out with it," she insisted, her deep blue eyes alight with mischief.

"I gather," he said slowly, looking from one woman to the other. "He was rather well into his cups."

Miss Hallowell nodded, "That goes without saying."

He blinked in surprise at her calm acceptance, then felt a rush of anger that something in her past should lead her to consider a man's drunkenness commonplace. He took a steadying breath. "It seems," he said evenly, "that the matter began with an altercation between himself and a watchman who was crying out the hour and saying all was well. Redinger didn't feel well, so he took exception to the man's statements."

"Boxing the watch," she stated, leaning back against a nest of gold brocade sofa pillows that highlighted the golden tones in her hair.

Miles wished he'd brought his portfolio to this visit. He would have delighted in sketching Miss Hallowell. A sketch of her nestled against the sofa pillows would have contrasted his sketch of Redinger against another bank of pillows.

"According to Redinger," he said slowly, "that was an accident. The box fell on him."

Ann Hallowell clapped her hands together and laughed. "Oh, famous! That, to be sure, was an accident!"

"I do so hope his injuries are not too severe," Mrs. Hallowell said, frowning slightly at her stepdaughter, condemning her amusement and too casual attitude. Miss Hallowell ignored her.

"No. It is my belief he is using cracked ribs and a broken arm as a formal excuse while bruises and scrapes on his face are more likely at fault," Miles said dryly.

Ann looked toward Mrs. Hallowell. "See what I mean about flaws?" She touched the scar on her chin. "Still believe he won't cry craven?"

Mrs. Hallowell looked chagrined. "But a man's vanity is a separate thing," she argued weakly.

A frown drew Miles' dusky-brown brows together. "I beg your pardon?" he asked.

"Oh, dear. I do apologize, Your Grace," Mrs. Hallowell said with a tittering laugh, her older woman manner at odds with her youthful appearance. "So rude of us. I will confess my mind is in a dither. Ours has a higher purpose," she stated meaningfully.

From the small sofa he heard a tiny spurt of laughter. Mrs. Hallowell quickly glanced in that direction, frowned, then continued. "We have planned this party carefully, balanced the guest list, and overall done our utmost to ensure its success and so to thereby convince the dowager not to hide herself and her art away from appreciative eyes. Now our numbers shall be uneven. What shall we do?"

She wrung her hands together a moment, then suddenly clasped them tightly together and surged to her feet. Miles perforce rose as well.

"I have it!" she exclaimed.

Ann and Miles looked at her curiously.

"You shall come to Versely Park in Viscount Redinger's stead!" Mrs. Hallowell exclaimed.

"Me?" protested Miles.

"Him?" protested Miss Hallowell.

They looked at each other. Ann shrugged.

"Yes. It is the perfect solution," Mrs. Hallowell insisted.

"Perfect solution?" Miles parroted, all at sea.

Ann Hallowell laughed. "Your course has been charted. Best you follow for Ursula will not take no for an answer once she's in full sail with an idea. I know. I've been her victim on more than one occasion."

Mrs. Hallowell paced the room, ignoring them both. "It is a perfect solution!" she murmured. "Well, not perfect perhaps. Perfect would be both attending. Under the circumstances, it is perfect . . . . Then again, maybe in all circumstances! Better suited, I'd hazard. Yes!"

"Mrs. Hallowell? . . ." Miles tried.

Ann chuckled. "No use. She is plotting and planning."

He cocked his head and his eyebrows rose in an expression that Ann began to see as his habit when he questioned another's statement. She owned it effective for she found herself hurrying to explain.

"When Ursula is planning something, particularly someone's life, she is lost to everything around her. She babbles to herself as if she were having a conversation, arguing points back and forth. When she is done, she will simply tell us what we are to do."

"Is there no arguing against her?" Miles asked.

"Oh, no. Words are useless," she said, laughter dancing in her eyes. "It's best to go along with her as much as one can. Objections are better through actions than words."

"Besides, you want to go, and she'd want you," Mrs. Hallowell chimed in, only pausing a moment in her pacing. "All that art . . . Did you know she has a Wingate?"

"No. Does she really?" Miles said with mild amusement. He hated to admit it, but she was correct. He did want to go to Versely Park. He had even felt a twinge of envy when Redinger mentioned it to him . . . But not at the behest of a scheming female! No matter what her plans. He'd had enough of those types in the days since he'd inherited the title.

Then again, her interest seemed to be more toward encouraging the Dowager Duchess to entertain more. Getting the Dowager to share her art collection was a worthwhile task. Perhaps he could offer some small support with their endeavor. The lump of cold dread he'd felt in his stomach when she decreed he come in Redinger's place began to dissolve. He began to feel more in charity with Mrs. Hallowell.

"A Wingate!" Ann exclaimed, chagrined. Ellinbourne! How could she have failed to connect his name? Wingate was one of her most favorite artists, one whose style she studied for her paintings. He'd complimented that schoolroom painting of hers and she'd just dismissed his words! She put her hands against her suddenly burning cheeks and rose hurriedly to her feet.

"I beg your pardon, Your Grace, I didn't connect your name . . . . And what you said of my painting . . . ." Ann knew she was babbling but couldn't stop. Like her grandmother, art was her passion. Now she understood why Ursula had been surprised when she didn't recognize the Duke of Ellinbourne's name!

He smiled at her, and Ann felt a frisson of excitement trail down her spine. The thought ran through her head that she wished he were Redinger, for she could see marrying a man like him.

Dismayed at her wayward thought, she dismissed it as quickly as it came.

"I'm used to people not connecting my name with my title, though I'll admit I've often wished it could be otherwise," Miles said with a slight laugh.

Ann's heart contracted painfully in her chest. She'd somehow wounded him and that was the last thing she could possibly have wished to do. Was it because no one equated Ellinbourne with Wingate? A duke with an artist?

"I have a present for you," he went on to say, banishing the twinge of bitterness she'd heard in his voice. "A sketch I did of Redinger that he bade me give to you."

"A sketch? How lovely. We must have it framed," Mrs. Hallowell said, this time not pausing in her pacing.

Miles and Ann ignored her, each too caught up in their painful awareness of the other.

"A real Wingate sketch?" Ann breathed, her eyes shining.

He paused. "I'm sorry, I signed it Ellinbourne," he said stiffly.

She shook her head. "What's the difference?"

"To many, everything."

"Nonsense," she swiftly declared. "It is the quality of the art, not the name upon it that is important."

"A duke patronizes art," he said for the second time that day, "he does not create it."

"Talent is talent. And I think you know that you only want reassurance from others," she said shrewdly.

Their eyes met and held each other's gaze. He shrugged finally, and a tiny smile pulled up the corner of his lips. "An artist's self-worth is measured in the appreciation of his endeavors in the eyes of others."

She considered his comment seriously. "To an extent. But are all capable of judgment?"

"Ah, there is the rub. Here." He handed her the scroll and sketch. "Redinger asked me to give you this to prove his disability, not as a work of art. On the scroll is, evidently, a poem written by him. He assures me that all women are enamored with poetry written for them.

Ann stared enraptured at the sketch, ignoring the scroll. She loved the picture. Not that it was of Redinger, who she supposed to be a bit of a spoiled youth, but because there was a wealth of emotion in the sketch, a wealth of unstated ideas. And because it was created by the man standing next to her. Her eyes glazed with unshed tears.

"Thank you," she choked out.

Miles saw the welling tears in her eyes. To his surprise, they were like a knife thrust in his gut. Damn Redinger. He was a lucky gentleman.

Ann laid a gentle hand on his arm. "You will come to Versely Park, won't you?" She knew that if he came, she would have someone she could talk to, and the pitying stares of the other guests would not bother her so.

He looked down into her wide open deep blue

eyes and could not imagine saying no. "May I escort you ladies?"

"Colonel Brantley, a friend of my stepmother's is, but we should be glad of another's company. We leave at nine. Is that too early?"

He laughed. "I am up regularly at dawn. I find it a most peaceful time to create. Nine will be fine. But aren't you going to read Redinger's poem? I'll admit I am curious. It was not an aspect of my cousin I'd expected to discover!"

"Yes, of course." She untied the purple ribbon and broke the seal on the scroll. It was tightly rolled and did not open easily.

Miles followed her as she crossed the room to lay the scroll out on the French-style writing desk so she could smooth it out. As she did so, her eyes scanned it. "Oh, dear," she said faintly, her cheeks burning.

"What is it?"

She stood aside to let him read the poem.

The Art of Love
by Sebastian Redinger, Viscount Redinger
O! Blue-ey'd dancing Sprite of Beauty
How you push and pull me from my duty.
A golden spirit chasing night's dew
With milk-white hands flutter'ng'afore you,
You catch my heart and parts with your motions
'Till my mind doth whirl and lose all notions.
And as lock doth joyfully meet the key
So my art doth strive to heed your plea.

Miles blanched, then dark color rose above his stock to stain his neck.

Redinger said he wrote it for an opera dancer. Miles should have deduced the poem would have a sexual nature, but for it to describe a sexual encounter and Redinger not remember the content was outrageous!

His fist closed about the parchment, his knuckles white. "Redinger!" he ground out.

Ursula stopped her pacing and turned to stare.

Miles stood rigidly a moment, a muscle jumping in his lean cheek as he worked to conquer his anger and chagrin. When he felt the flush of color and embarrassment fade, he turned to look at Miss Hallowell standing so still beside him. Her complexion blanched white, her dark blue eyes wide with shock.

If Redinger had been there, Miles would have happily throttled him.

Then he saw something begin to displace the shock in her eyes. Ann Hallowell looked up at him. A mischievous smile turned up her lips and lit her eyes where only moments before shock had dwelt.

He raised his hand to halt her words before she even thought to say them. "This is my office, and I shall take great pleasure in stuffing it down his throat."

She laughed. "At least it rhymed."

CHAPTER 4
THE POEM

Miles pushed past Redinger's butler even before that worthy had time to realize who stood at the door.

"Sebastian!" Miles called up the stairs as he impatiently flung off his greatcoat and hat, scattering water droplets across the marble floor, and thrust them into the butler's arms. He bounded up the stairs, taking the steps two at a time. "Sebastian!"

Anger and embarrassment coursed through his blood and throbbed at his temples. Cousin or not, or perhaps because he was his cousin, Miles wanted to haul Sebastian out of his nest of bordello red velvet and white lace to blacken his other eye. The look on Miss Hallowell's face after she'd read the poem stayed fresh in his mind and twisted into his gut. Though obviously a woman of humor, gifting her with bawdy doggerel insulted this gracious and beautiful creature.

"Sebastian!" he bellowed as he slammed open his cousin's bedroom door. The door banged against the mahogany dresser, sloshing water out of a porcelain wash bowl.

His fists clenched, Miles strode into the room. "Sebastian, I ought to—" He stopped short. Sebastian was not alone. Two dandies with impossibly high neckcloths and tight fitting, wasp-waisted padded jackets leaned against the bedposts.

"Miles!" Sebastian said happily. "Didn't expect to see you again today. Do you know Chester Harley and Jerry Jessup?" he asked, indicating the two gentlemen.

"Pleased, Your Grace," Jerry Jessup said. Chester Harley bobbed his head. Jessup whacked Harley in the stomach with the back of his hand. "Say something, you great noddy! He's a duke, ya' know."

"Oof. Yes, pleased, Your Grace," Harley squeaked out.

"Hello," Miles said shortly, scarcely glancing at the two men, his attention focused on Sebastian Redinger. "Excuse me, gentlemen." He crossed in front of the men and grabbed Sebastian by the front of his banyan, pulling him up until he sat upright.

"What? Ouch! Ouch! Ah-- The ribs! Easy cuz," protested Sebastian, his face inches from Miles's.

"I say, old man," protested Jerry Jessup.

"Your Grace!" protested Randolph from the dressing room doorway.

"How dare you send a woman like Miss Hallowell a piece of bawdy doggerel," Miles demanded, shaking Sebastian.

"Ouch! Ack! Damn, Miles, what are you talking about?" Sebastian gasped out. He batted at Miles' grip with his good hand.

"Your Grace, please!" Randolph exclaimed, crossing the room to the bed, his hands worrying together.

Miles let go of Sebastian's nightshirt and disgustedly shoved his back against his pillows. "What am I talking about? You have the temerity to ask what I'm talking about?" He pulled the wrinkled poem from his waistband and tossed it on the bed. "This is what I'm talking about," he said, gesturing at the crumbled square of paper.

"My poem?" Sebastian said, confused.

"You wrote a poem?" crowed Jessup, snatching it off the counterpane.

"Oh dear," murmured Randolph.

"Yes," Miles said, turning to glare at Sebastian's butler. "*Oh, dear,* is correct." He turned back to Sebastian. "You insulted a lady with that poem, a lady you claim you're going to marry. A very beautiful and gracious lady, too."

"*A golden spirit chasing night's dew,*" Jessup read dramatically.

Harley leaned over his shoulder. "What, no day jollys? Tsk tsk."

"*With milk-white hands flutter'ng 'afore you, you catch my heart,*" Jessup laid his hand over his heart, "*and parts,*" he emphasized, thrusting his hips forward.

"Oooo," Chester Harley said, then fell back against the bed, giggling.

"That's enough." Miles grabbed the poem out of Jessup's hands and ripped it into pieces.

"Dash it, Miles, I didn't remember it to be raw," Sebastian protested.

"Dew, oh, I like that!" Harley said, wiping his streaming eyes as he struggled to contain his laughter. "Better'n 'seed' or 'cum'. Hang me, Sebastian, if you ain't got real poetry talent," he said earnestly.

Sebastian struggled up on to his good elbow. "Do you really think so? I think I turn a word well, but that's just me, ya' know," he said eagerly.

"What?" protested Miles, anger giving ground to astonishment.

Jessup nodded. "Harley's got the right of it. You're a dab hand. You could give that Byron fellow competition with the ladies."

"Are you all mad?" Miles asked, looking from one man to the other. Their expressions were quite serious.

"Oh, I ain't saying this was a poem for a lady," Jerry Jessup conceded, rocking back on his heels.

Harley frowned consideringly as he nodded. "Dare say Sebastian here just got caught up in the beauty of the words and didn't think none of the meaning." He leaned forward and tapped Miles on the arm. "Sometimes arty folk don't, ya' know," he confided.

Miles groaned and sank down onto a chair by the bed. He put his head in his hands. They were all mad, without an ounce of sense!

Sebastian drummed his fingers on the bed. "I'll write Miss Hallowell a new poem," he decided. "A better one."

Miles lifted his head. "I should hope it would be a better one," he said, then muttered, "though I've no expectations."

"Just for that, I'll show you. I'll write her a poem every day, see if I don't," Sebastian huffed and looked away from his cousin.

"That's the ticket," Harley said.

Jessup nodded as he planted his hands on his wasp-waist and stared at Miles.

Miles grimaced. "My apologies for offending. I am hardly one to stand in an artist's way," he acknowledged. He sighed heavily, then looked steadily at his cousin. "Just promise me something, Sebastian. Humor me, really."

"What?" Sebastian turned to look back at Miles,

his battered face looking as sullen and resentful as a five-year old child.

"Send the poems to me first," Miles said.

Sebastian frowned. "That's a might high, cuz. Just 'cause you're an artist doesn't mean you know poetry."

"No?" Miles surged to his feet, feeling more irritated with his cousin than he could ever remember feeling. "Well, I can recognize bawdy lines when I read them," he retorted as he paced the room.

"Ouch," Jerry Jessup murmured. Chester Harley nodded.

Sebastian flushed. "That was an accident. I mistook the poem is all. No harm," he said, his fingers plucking at the folds of his covers.

"No harm? You weren't the one standing in front of the lady when she read the poem. No, you want to send her more poetry, you send it to me first."

"Dash it, Miles, that'd waste time. Miss Hallowell is leaving tomorrow," Sebastian protested.

Miles stopped and faced his cousin. "I know.' He laughed and ran his right hand through his hair. "I'm accompanying her!"

"You? Why?" Sebastian exclaimed.

"Mrs. Hallowell decided I could be useful."

"Useful?" Chester Harley asked, fascinated.

Miles twisted his lips, then nodded. "First," he explained, counting on one finger, "I'm to keep your seat warm at dinner and thereby maintain the guest numbers and mix. Second," another finger joined the first, "I gather I'm to lend my voice to suggestions for how she makes her art collection available for viewing in some museum or other establishment."

"Your Grace," Randolph exclaimed, "Surely you cannot wish to attend this house party in the middle of season!" His long face looked more pinched than normal.

"On the contrary," Miles drawled, "Escaping London at this time of year seems eminently desirable."

Harley nodded sympathetically. "Getting cornered by match-making mamas, I warrant."

Worse. More like match-making relatives.

CHAPTER 5

THE JOURNEY

Miles leaned back against the cushions of the well-appointed Hallowell carriage and wondered for the tenth time how he got himself into this. He knew he was drawn by the art of Versely Park. The Duchess of Malmsby was well known for her art collection and, like a boy anticipating a special show or treat, he felt a child-like anticipation of seeing her extensive art collection.

Across from him sat Miss Hallowell and her stepmother. No two women could have been more different. Mrs. Hallowell was vivacious and giggly like a young girl. Miss Hallowell, more serious, did not sparkle like her stepmother; however, there was a sunshine warmth and comfortableness about her, a centeredness that attracted Miles.

He did wonder at Mrs. Hallowell's marriage to Miss Hallowell's father, as she could not have been more than five to seven years older than her stepdaughter. Even Mrs. Hallowell's escort, Colonel Brantley, who sat next to him, appeared a good two decades older than Mrs. Hallowell. Odd pair on the surface; however, they appeared quite contented in each other's company and, for that, Miles envied their situation. He hoped to one day achieve a similar comfort with his chosen bride. If he was allowed to choose and not be harangued by relatives as to who was the proper wife for his title.

He couldn't see Miss Hallowell married to his cousin Sebastian. Sebastian would naturally be drawn to someone like Mrs. Hallowell. But it was not his issue and if Miss Hallowell was content with the match he wished her the best of life.

Colonel Brantley and Mrs. Hallowell kept up a lively banter, or more accurately, Mrs. Hallowell kept up a lively banter and everyone else listened, nodded, or murmured the appropriate agreeable words.

Only Miss Hallowell appeared decidedly uncomfortable from her place across from him. She didn't know where to look, like she was embarrassed to see him and that disappointed him. He felt oddly drawn to this woman, his cousin's near fiancé. Was it the dark honey color of her hair, her wide blue eyes, or that crescent scar on her chin that so intrigued him? He couldn't say. Maybe it was just that sense of serenity in her manner that he enjoyed.

The trip to Versely Park was long, but he was glad that he'd had his coach sent ahead with his valet and groomsmen. He did not think he would be riding back in the same carriage with the Hallowell's. He much preferred his own carriage and definitely not sitting with his back to the driver.

That last stray thought brought a smile to his lips. Before his elevated position in life, sitting with his back to the driver was all he ever did and took as expected, or sitting atop a mailcoach with other paying passengers who could not afford inside passage.

"Ann," Ursula suddenly said, shifting toward her

stepdaughter, "when was the last time you saw your grandmother's art collection? Have you ever seen it in its entirety?"

Ann laughed. "I doubt that I've seen everything in it. I've seen different pieces of it, as what she has on display often changes. I doubt Grandmother has ever seen it in its entirety, as she is always acquiring and storing away. These days my cousin Aidan does most of the actual acquiring for her."

"Aidan Nowlton buys for your grandmother? I know he owns a gallery just off Mayfair, but I wouldn't have taken him for one of the buyers' agents for a collection like the Duchess has. Art buying can be quite cut throat," Miles said.

Ann's eyes sparkled as she looked across at him. "Do not be taken in by my cousin's air of ennui. But in truth, grandmother has used many in the family for her art acquisition."

"Yes, I remember when you went to Sicily with your grandmother, your Aunt Catherine, and cousin Helena, after your father's death," Ursula said.

Ursula looked over at Miles. "That was to be Ann's come out year. During her mourning, or rather because of her mourning, her grandmother decided to take her on her planned trip to Sicily, to buy art from someone."

She looked back at Ann, her growing agitation at the memories evident in her posture and rising tone. "That your grandmother had no concern for your, or your cousin's safety with that beast Napoleon ruling Italy, is beyond comprehension."

"The kingdom was under British Protection," Ann gently reminded her. This had long been a contentious subject. "Lord William Bentinck was there.

And we were with my aunt and uncle, and remember, Uncle William was with the Home Office."

Ann looked over at Miles. "Lady Travis offered grandmother the opportunity to buy her entire art collection before she contacted galleries and other collectors. Of course, my grandmother quite readily agreed and we were off to Sicily within days of her receiving Lady Travis's letter."

Miles laughed, "So that is where Lady Travis's art collection went! Many wondered what she did with her paintings when she decided to travel the world."

"Yes, they knew each other from their come-out days and stayed correspondence friends when Lady Travis and her husband moved to Sicily. After her husband's death, she said she could no longer stay where she had so many wonderful memories. She decided to make new wonderful memories, so when she made the decision to dispose of all her belongings and travel, she contacted grandmother."

"Still, to have you girls go there at that time, I shudder at what might have occurred." Lady Hallowell shivered slightly at the thought and Colonel Brantley reached across to gently pat her knee.

"Had I been with you at the time, and not at my parents' home, I would have forbade it as your stepmother," she righteously declared.

Ann laughed. "That would have been a waste of words. And nothing bad occurred, at least to us. And in some ways, it was fortuitous, as we were there to give Lady Blessingame condolences and support when she lost her husband so suddenly. They had been married less than a year, you know."

"Harry Blessingame?" Colonel Brantley asked. "Fine fellow, worked with the foreign office. Great loss to the nation."

"Lord Blessingame was a spy? It was rumored he died because of his spy activities." Ann said.

Colonel Brantley squirmed a bit and compressed his lips. "I wouldn't use the term spy. But what did you gels do with that art? I wouldn't have thought you would be involved with the packing and crating."

Ann recognized Colonel Brantley's discomfort with the mention of spy activities and changed the subject. She would love to have teased more information from the Colonel as she and Helena had wondered about the nature of Lord Blessingame's death, but she allowed herself to be diverted.

"Boring things. We sorted and catalogued Lady Travis's collection and worked with grandmother to decide what would go directly to Versely Park and what they might send on to Aidan's gallery for immediate sale. She did have some highly valuable pieces, like the two framed Michelangelo sketches that people appear interested in seeing. They were complimentary pieces, part of a study for a larger painting."

"Lady Travis said she bought the sketches from a landed gentleman in Italy, right before Napoleon took over. Lady Travis said she would have liked to have gotten more works of art out of the country, but they had to leave in a hurry to avoid Napoleon's army."

She looked across at Miles. "Your Grace, I believe that is also when Lady Travis acquired one of your uncle's paintings as well."

"Lady Travis had a Clarence Wingate?" asked Miles, surprised.

"Yes. It was a very large painting of a young man."

Suddenly Ann felt her cheeks getting warm as she remembered the subject matter of that painting. Across from her, the Duke, seeing her blush, smiled and laughed gently.

"I think I know that painting. So your grandmother has it. It has been a family mystery for some time as to what happened to that painting."

"Well, that's the thing. I don't believe it did make it back to England, though I know we put in it with the stacks of paintings that were going to be sent to Grandmother."

"Knowing the subject matter as I do, could your grandmother have kept if from the eyes of others?"

"What are you two talking about?" asked Ursula.

"A painting by Clarence Wingate. Lady Blessingame told us it was a portrait of one of his nephews," Ann told her stepmother.

"Yes," said Miles, "my cousin Adam, now the Earl of Norwalk, and he has been looking for that painting for years, ever since he reached his majority and understood that his uncle had sold it when he promised he never would."

"My cousin, Helena, who is a sculptress, was quite taken with the painting. I know she snuck back into the painting storage room to make sketches. She said this was the closest she could get to studying the male form, and she was not going to allow the opportunity to pass by."

Miles nodded. "I imagine for a woman to get models is impossible."

"It is quite an interesting painting," Ann said archly. "I can understand why he would like it back."

Miles harrumphed as he glanced out the window at the rural scenery. "He doesn't want it back for the reason you think," he said, remembering his cousin's fury when their uncle nonchalantly said he'd sold it to buy more art supplies. He turned back to look at her. "He wants the painting back so he can burn it."

"Burn it! Heavens no! It is too beautiful a painting to be burned."

"It is," Miles nodded, then laughed. "However, the Earl takes great exception to being depicted as the biblical Adam with an apple in his hand. I can't say as I blame him."

"Gracious!" said Ursula, "I can understand that if he were painted in the *altogether*. Does your grandmother display it?" Ursula asked uncomfortably.

"Grandmother doesn't have the painting, as far as I know," Ann said.

"Intriguing," said Miles. "Does she have any idea where it went? I know my cousin would want to know."

"No, it was one of the things she commented on when we returned from Sicily that the painting did not come to Versely Park and Aidan said he did not have it either," Ann said.

"Did she suspect it was stolen?" Miles asked.

"I don't know; however, it is a rather large painting to be stolen."

"That is true. I only saw it once. I'm afraid the cousins teased Adam about it without mercy. That contributed to his hatred for the painting," Miles admitted. He considered. "It could have been removed from the frame and rolled up. That would make it easier to steal."

Ann nodded. "I could see that occurring. We weren't around when the artworks were shipped. We left when the villa carpenter was still building crates."

"At least I can inform Adam of its last known whereabouts," Miles said.

Miles would have liked to continue the conversation about the missing painting; however, at that moment the carriage rolled into the forecourt of Versely Park.

Looking at the estate house, Colonel Brantley grunted. "This ain't no manor house."

Mrs. Hallowell laughed merrily. "No, Mr. Hallowell told me the oldest parts of the building date the fifteenth century."

"Yes," Ann said as she looked out the carriage window with affection at the house. "It was originally a monastery that saw its demise under Henry VIII. Henry gave the property to Edmund Versely. Versely built a fortified manor house around the monastery. Later owners just added to it with whatever architecture style was popular at that time," she explained.

Miles studied the building. It had to be the ugliest building he had ever seen.

Sensing his perturbation, Mrs. Hallowell wrinkled her nose. "It's not an attractive house."

"Not on the outside," Ann agreed, "but it is quite fascinating inside."

"What Ann means is it's easy to get lost." Mrs. Hallowell said as the carriage rolled to a halt and a footman ran forward to open the carriage door.

"And have you?" Miles asked as he descended from the carriage and offered his hand to Miss Hallowell.

"What?" Mrs. Hallowell asked as she took his hand next.

"Have you ever gotten lost in the house?"

"Truthfully no, as every time I visited, I was with my husband, but I have been told others have."

"Only at large house parties where getting lost and stumbling into a wrong room was part of the game," Ann said as the party walked toward the front of the house.

"Ann!" Mrs. Hallowell protested.

Ann laughed, "That's what Grandmother always says."

"Well, I should hope that is not something she is expecting at this house party."

"What am I not expecting?" said a voice from the doorway.

Two elderly women stood on the massive single stone stoop. Miles recognized the woman with the purple turban as Lady Oakley. He assumed the other was the Dowager Duchess of Malmsby.

"Grandmother!" Ann cried out, running to her grandmother, who opened her arms to her as she would a small child. Ann clasped her tightly, then stood back. "I have missed you so."

"And I you! I believe you know my friend, Lady Oakley."

"Yes, I attended a musicale at her home in April."

"It was a wonderful squeeze, was it not?" Lady Oakley said, affectionately taking both of Ann's hands in hers.

Ann smiled. "Indeed. Quite enjoyable."

The Duchess held out her hand to Mrs. Hallowell. "So nice to see you again, Ursula, and you as well, Colonel Brantley."

Though not in any way related to the Malmsby family, they welcomed Ursula into their fold for their love of Ann.

"But Grandmother, let me introduce you to—"

"No need! I would recognize a Redinger! I have known the family for years."

"But this is not---" Ann protested.

"No!" Mrs. Hallowell said.

Lady Oakley grabbed Ann's arm. When Ann looked up at her, the woman shook her head no slightly to both Ann and Mrs. Hallowell. "Nice to see you again, Lord Redinger," she said heartily.

"But—" Mrs. Hallowell began again.

"You must be tired after your long drive. Mrs. Weaver will show you to your rooms," Lady Oakley said, quickly cupping Ann and Mrs. Hallowell's elbows in her palms to lead them to the stairs.

"But Redinger—"

"Yes, yes," I know," Lady Oakley said heartily. "Standing here in the hall is not a time for discussion. Much better when you have freshened up and rested, isn't that right, Vivian?" Lady Oakley said over her shoulder at their hostess.

"Yes, and resting sounds like a wonderful idea," the Duchess said. "I think I shall do so as well this afternoon."

"Excellent idea for all of us!" Lady Oakley enthused.

"Now see here, Lady Oakley," Miles began.

"Not now, Lord Redinger. We shall all meet again before dinner and have a comfortable coze. And you shall meet the other guests as well. We shall have a delightful house party together, I know."

"Ah, there you are Mrs. Weaver! Is everything ready for my guests?" the Duchess asked as the housekeeper descended the stairs.

"Yes, Your Grace," said the housekeeper, curtsying. She looked across the hall at Miles and Colonel Brantley. "Donna shall show the gentlemen to their rooms," she said with stately formality from her place on the stairs.

The maid at her side curtsied and came down the stairs to greet Miles and Colonel Brantley. "If you gentlemen will follow me, I shall get you settled in a tick," the cheery maid said.

Colonel Brantley and Miles looked at each other. Colonel Brantley shrugged. Miles compressed his lips in a tight line. While he may not care for being a duke and the toadying that went with it, he also did not wish to be taken for a member of Aunt Suzanne's brood and though Sebastian was a friend as well as his cousin, he particularly wouldn't want to be Sebastian.

It was obvious Lady Oakley did not want to correct the Duchess and instead wanted him to agree to the charade. But why? Lady Oakley was known for her eccentricities; however, this was too outlandish even for her.

He followed the little country maid up the wide carpeted steps, Colonel Brantley following behind.

CHAPTER 6

BEING THE VISCOUNT

Miles quickly stopped thinking of Lady Oakley and her odd behavior as he came to see the art work hung along the staircase going up the stairs, and in the long gallery they walked down to a bedroom wing closer to the older parts of the house. Each painting was worth at least ten to fifteen minutes of intense study.

Despite his misgivings about coming to Versely, and the Duchess's odd behavior, Miles knew if he had time to study even a tenth of the paintings he saw, he would be content with the house party.

At the end of the long gallery, the maid, Donna, pushed open a set of white double doors accented with gold leaf trim.

"Your Grace, this will be your apartment," she said as she led them into a large parlor. To the left is your bedchamber and, beyond that, your bath. Your valet has the small room here on the right, so you will not need to ring a bell for him.

Miles circled the room once, then looked in the bedroom on the left where she had indicated. It was a comparable size to the parlor and bigger than many of the cottages a tenant farmer and his family lived in.

"This is fine, thank you."

"I quite agree," Colonel Brantley said, rocking back on his heels.

"It was the suite reserved for a royal visit," Donna explained.

"Has any royalty stayed here?" Miles asked with a laugh.

Donna giggled and quickly raised her hand to cover her mouth.

"No, she said impishly, "but we are prepared!"

"I should say so," Miles said, looking about the room again.

"Colonel Brantley, sir, you are just down the hall here. If you would please follow me?" the maid said, opening the double doors again.

"Yes, yes, of course," Brantley said.

When they left, Miles turned to look back at his assigned quarters for his stay. The décor was heavy purple velvet and gold brocade lavishly trimmed with gold bullion fringe. If the colors had been red instead of purple and gold, the flamboyance to the décor would have fit for a bawd house. Oddly, however, it all worked together, even to the paintings that hung along the walls and over the fireplace, portraits of former kings and queens of England all garbed in purple, gold, or black. The coffered ceiling was elaborately carved with painted medallions in the squares between the crosspieces that depicted astrological constellations.

He walked to the window and drew the drapes aside to look out.

The room overlooked a formal garden with neat walkways and precisely trimmed hedges. Compared to the inside of the house, with its display of art along almost every square inch of wall space, the exterior gardens appeared austere. Perhaps that was the idea. A breath of fresh air after the ornate, complicated interior décor.

His cousin would have adored the opulence. Miles found it stifling.

~

MR. WILLIAM BERRYMAN, Miles's valet, arrived an hour later. Two footmen followed him into the suite of rooms, each carrying a handle of this largest trunk.

Miles's lips twitched at seeing the men struggle with the trunk. Clothes did not make up the weight of the trunk. Art supplies did. These jackets, pantaloons, and waistcoats could have fit in a portmanteau, Berryman packed his smalls and carefully starched cravats in the portmanteau he carried. From a clothing standpoint, Miles always traveled light. The same could not be true for the tools of his passion.

When they set the trunk down, Miles's thanked the footmen for their efforts, winked, and slipped them a small thank you.

"You should not do that, Your Grace," remonstrated his valet. "That can only lead to surly behavior if no gratuity is received."

"Not toward me," Miles said.

"No, that is a bad precedent! Others will be compared and found lacking."

Miles considered his man's comment. "I can see that." He sat down on a purple velvet side chair. "But I believe I will continue to do so. That can be considered the Duke's eccentricity. I've been where they are. Though I have always been around those blessed with titles, I am a clergyman's son first. The precepts taught by my father do not disappear with an elevation in status! If I can influence my peers to follow my example, so much the better, I'd say."

Miles sat in silence for a moment while his valet began to unpack his trunk. His head canted to one side. "I just realized how that maid addressed me!" he exclaimed. He stood up.

"Beg pardon, Your Grace," said his valet.

"That's how she addressed me, as Your Grace. How could she know I am a duke if the Duchess and Lady Oakley addressed me as Viscount Redinger?"

"Your Grace?" repeated the valet. He paused in withdrawing items from the trunk to look at Miles, troubled.

Miles laughed as he paced the room. "Those old biddies were making a May Game of me! I wonder why? Should I play this out?"

"Your Grace?" squeaked his man.

"Yes, I think I will. That will quite surprise them. I will need to bring Miss Hallowell into my plans. William, for the nonce, I am no longer Duke of Ellinbourne, I am Viscount Redinger. See that you address me as my lord, not Your Grace until such time as the Duchess is done with her game."

"Not address you as Your Grace? But—"

"I insist. Address me as my lord. Come on. Say it."

"If you insist, my—my lord."

"Excellent! Good job," Miles said, rubbing his hands together. "Here," he said, handing his man a coin. "This should sweeten the effort."

"Your—my lord!" protested the valet.

"Have you unpacked my sketchbook and charcoal yet?"

The valet mutely gathered them from a bureau top and handed them to Miles.

"Thank you. I think I shall walk around to stretch out my legs for a bit."

"Is there any outfit you would like me to set out for dinner tonight?"

"No, whatever. You have better taste than I do as to the niceties of a peer's attire, that's why I hired you. Carry on," Miles said as he crossed the room to the door.

"Yes, my lord."

~

ANN HAD BEEN STEWING like cook's beef bone broth for the past hour until she could stand it no longer. Her stepmother was in the suite of rooms down the hall. Ann determinedly entered Ursula's sitting room. "Ursula! How could you?" she exclaimed, arms akimbo as she watched her stepmother placidly laid the book she'd been reading beside her and lean back against the cushions of the settee.

"How could I what?" Ursula asked with contrived, wide-eyed innocence.

"Faugh! You know what! Allow Grandmother to believe the Duke of Ellinbourne was Viscount Redinger!"

"It would be embarrassing for the Duchess to call her out in such a public manner. I could not do that, and you saw how Lady Oakley understood that immediately. I took my lead on how to respond from that dear lady."

"Now grandmother will be pushing us together at every opportunity. We must correct her!"

"Me, correct the Dowager Duchess of Malmsby? I would not dare."

"Ursula, you are being impossible! If you won't, then I shall."

"No, Ann. You haven't seen your grandmother in nigh a year. You don't know where her mind is. What if she is truly becoming senile? If you are that concerned, I would bring the matter up with Lady Oakley first."

"But what about the Duke? Isn't it insulting if everyone calls him my lord instead of Your Grace?"

Ursula waved a hand airily. "He has not been a duke that long, and he was not raised to the manner."

"Aargh!" Ann exclaimed, frustrated that she could not make her stepmother perceive how egregious an error it was to call the Duke *Viscount Redinger*. She crossed to the window and blindly stared out at the grounds of Versely Park, trying to come up with an argument that would sway Ursula.

She shook her head for she could think of nothing. She looked closely at the garden grounds that led to the old abbey wing. The Duke of Ellinbourne was out there with his sketchbook.

"I will talk to the Duke and get his opinion on how this should proceed. I see him in the garden now. If I hurry, I can catch him before he wanders elsewhere," she said.

"Don't forget your bonnet," was all Ursula said as she picked up a book to continue reading.

Ann hurried back to her room, grabbing up a shawl and her a straw bonnet. She lightly ran down the stair, holding the bonnet on her head by hanging on to the untied bonnet ribbons. She slowed down long enough to throw the shawl around her shoulders before she went out the terrace doors in the drawing room. Her weak ankle only protested her pace with a couple of sharp twinges as she hurried down the path that led to the abbey.

At least it didn't threaten to give out on her as it had done a few times in the past.

She slowed down when she saw the duke, sitting on the ground, leaning against a tree trunk as he sketched the abbey building. He'd taken his jacket off and rolled up his sleeves as he sketched. She saw him absently brush a lock of light brown hair back off his forehead with his left hand while his right hand moved smoothly and swiftly across the paper. Now that she had found him, Ann was not certain how to proceed.

Dare she interrupt him? She started to take a step backward to leave him in peace when he looked over and saw her.

He smiled, set his sketching materials aside and rose to his feet.

"You have caught me," he said. He withdrew a handkerchief from his subdued, light gray waistcoat to wipe the dust from his drawing charcoal off of his fingers. "After several hours riding in a carriage I had to get out and stretch my legs and for me, such activities always lead to a sketch or two." He looked up at the partially derelict Abbey wing of the house. "I felt compelled," he confessed, scowling up at the building.

Ann laughed. "That is nothing to be ashamed of, Your Grace! I wish I had the same driving compulsion. While I enjoy creating drawings and paintings, I am a mere dabbler compared to you."

He shrugged. "My compulsion to draw has been compared to a compulsive gambler or compulsive imbiber of strong spirits. Addictions to rise above," he said, thinking of his uncle's attitude toward his art.

"What?" Ann exclaimed. She marched over to stand in front of him. She dropped her bonnet ribbons and raised her hand to shake a reprimanding finger at him. "You are indulging in a fit of blue megrims and that will not do. Especially not in this household! The Malmsbys—No, the extended Nowlton family worship creativity and the arts. For many of us, such as myself, the lack of a shining talent raises little monsters of jealousy. If a person has a talent, it behooves them to use it! God does not pass out talents willy-nilly. If there are those that say you should put your paint pots away, then they are merely jealous."

Miss Hallowell's intense ferocity drew a smile from Miles. He crossed his arms over his chest and tilted his head down to look at her as she railed at him. He had been indulging in a bit of self-pity, and she was right to call him on it.

Ever since he had inherited the ducal coronet, he had felt prodded, poked, abjured, and hounded to be other than he was. He didn't have a problem with being a duke. With good advisers and staff, the estate and the monies derived from the estate and the investments required little from him. A word here and there, a nod, a thank you, and everything ran like clockwork. He did not understand why he needed to change who he was though most of his family argued he should. Of course, they also had known Uncle Clarence, a brilliant artist, but a reckless man up to every rig that presented itself. He partied as often as he could find a party and was known to have fluid romantic entanglements.

Sometimes Miles thought that is what his relatives feared the most, that Miles would follow his uncle's lead into a debauched lifestyle.

They didn't realize there was no chance of that. He was a churchman's son and well versed in proper behavior. Some would hold that was all the more reason for him to rebel and be like his uncle; however, that was not Miles. Never would be, which he supposed made him a dull dog. He'd learned art from his uncle, not life skills.

Suddenly he realized Miss Hallowell was silent and staring up at him, a frown creasing her forehead.

"I beg your pardon, Miss Hallowell, I fell to woolgathering, one of my many faults. I am not well-mannered, as my Aunt Suzanne, Redinger's mother, tells me too often to ignore," he said with a smile and a laugh. He ran a hand through his hair, combing it back with his fingers. One wave of hair insisted on flopping forward.

He bent over to pick up his sketch pad and paper wrapped stick of charcoal from the ground. "Tell me, Miss Hallowell, about this part of Versely Park. Is this the wing the Dowager Duchess is thinking to make into a museum?" he asked. He held out his arm to her.

She placed her hand in the crook of his elbow and let him lead her closer to the building. "Partly," she said.

"The section where the roof and floor collapsed happened long ago during Cromwell's time. I imagine the abbey was quite striking in its day, but not favored by the Roundheads. They looted and vandalized this section, little understanding that it was this square building addition off the abbey that was where the wealth of the abbey resided."

She looked up at the awkward additions and bits and bobs that had been added to the house over the centuries. "When the first Duke of Malmsby was granted the property, they accepted it with ill-hidden disgust, for they found it in disrepair and quite uninteresting from an architectural standpoint. However, after taking possession and beginning the task of shoring up the shared wall with the vandalized abbey, they discovered paintings, sculptures, gems, all manner of ecclesiastical riches hidden in the walls. We don't know if the wealth was all the monks, or if other churches gave their wealth to the monks for safe keeping. No one has ever come forward to inquire about anything. Needless to say, it wasn't the treasure they'd hoped to find."

"Interesting." Miles stared up at the house with a vision of how it must have looked in the past. "What happened to the monks?" he asked.

"Murdered, we believe, but we don't know where the bodies might be and we have never had anyone claim ghosts haunt the property." She shrugged. "We don't know. However, it did make for some fun family storytelling!"

"My cousin Lancelot has the most creative mind. When I was younger, the cousins would gather here in the summer to visit Grandmother and Grandfather. We used to take turns making up the most outlandish history for the family and the property. Lancelot's stories were always the best. The most Gothic in nature, like *The Castle of Otranto*. With all the stories I've heard over the years, I don't think I would recognize the truth if it were told to me!"

Miles stopped suddenly, nearly over balancing Ann. "Look, he said softly, pointing to the ruined abbey. "What do you see?"

Ann cocked her head, unsure what it was she was supposed to be seeing. Then the clouds shifted.

Late afternoon sunlight played across the stone blocks with its open roof and empty window arches. A palette of color shone on the rock face. There were greens, blues, and purples, along with pinks, yellows, and oranges. The gray stone hid behind the color thrown at them by the sun, and black hid in tiny crevices.

"I should think to try to paint that would be an exercise in futility. How could one layout color as vivid as we see here and have people believe those are the colors seen?" Ann asked.

"I think we should try," Miles said.

"We?" Ann asked, startled.

"Yes, we can come out here in late afternoon, before the sun does its sunset show, and create our sketches in preparation for the colors."

"It doesn't do this every day, you know."

"Of course not! That is what will make it fun. And if we don't get the colors we want, we can still sketch and mix other colors and discuss composition."

"You would want to paint with me?" Ann asked.

"Of course! You are quite talented, for all you are self-taught. That is obvious in that little painting you stepmother likes. You just want a little suggestion here, a nudge there, to release your talent. That is what my uncle did for me, and I can do it for you." He said, quite pleased with his idea.

Ann recognized his pleasure in his own idea; however, she did not know that she felt the same pleasure he did! While he was an artist, she was a dabbler. She would rather watch him create than for him to waste time trying to teach her.

"Your Grace, I—" she began.

"Yoo-hoo! Viscount Redinger!" called out Lady Oakley. She stood on the terrace and waved at him. Even at the distance across the grounds Miles could tell she was smiling. She fairly bounced as she waved to them.

Ann dropped his arm as they turned to face Lady Oakley.

Ann huffed; her mouth set in a straight line. She crossed her arms over her chest. "She knows you are not Redinger," she said crossly.

He nodded. "I'll warrant your grandmother does as well." He slid a sideways glance at Ann. "I think your grandmother and Lady Oakley are up to some mischief," he murmured.

"Why do you say that?"

"When the maid, Donna, showed me to my rooms —the suite reserved for royalty, I might add—she called me Your Grace."

"You're in the purple passion suite!" Ann exclaimed. "That is what my cousins and I called that suite."

A laugh burbled up inside her, then she finally broke into uncontrollable laughter.

"What? What is it?" he asked.

"You are probably right as to mischief," Ann said as she struggled to get her laughter under control. "I should have realized she has been good for too long!"

"I don't understand," Miles said.

"My grandmother loves pranks. Not nasty ones, but fun ones. She was always thinking up pranks to pull on her grandchildren when we were growing up," Ann explained as Miles smiled and waved back at Lady Oakley.

"We should probably be heading back to the main house anyway. The wind is picking up and there is the beginning of a chill in the air," he said as he put on his jacket.

It impressed Ann that he could shrug into his coat without the assistance of his valet.

"The maid, I believe her name is Donna," he continued, "addressed me as 'Your Grace'. I did not tumble to the import of that action until an hour later. If the staff knows I am not Redinger, then I believe your grandmother does as well. So, I've decided to play along," he said as they walked back to the house and Lady Oakley.

Lady Oakley tried to wave them to her at a faster pace; however, Miles chose to ignore that bit of body language and take his time with Miss Hallowell. He enjoyed her company.

"What do you mean?"

"I shall answer to Redinger."

"But you're a duke! That's so disrespectful!"

"Perhaps it would be if I had been raised to the expectation, but I wasn't. I am a clergyman's son."

"You have said that before. Do you hold that as some trump card?"

"I suppose in a way I do. It is my way of honoring my father and not allowing myself to become caught up in the title and lose my sense of perspective with those around me." He laughed. "Too many others do that for me!"

The twilight breeze quickened. Treetops swayed and garden flowers bent before it. The chilling breeze snatched Ann's untied bonnet from her head.

"Oh!" Ann whirled around to try to catch a ribbon, but the wind sent the bonnet twenty feet away before dumping it to the ground and rolling it over and over.

Miles thrust his sketchbook into Ann's hands and ran to rescue the bonnet. When first he stooped to pick up a ribbon, the wind playfully skittered it out of his reach. He quickly moved again to the capture the errant headgear and planted his boot on the end of the ribbon to lay claim before the wind could play again.

When he turned back to look at Ann, he found his breath caught in his chest. While the wind had played with Ann's bonnet, it had played with Ann's hair as well. Strands whipped free of their confining pins and framed her face in a riot of dark blond curls and waves. This would be a portrait worth painting, he decided, not some staid formal sitting. She was beautiful. Not in the London marriage mart diamond-of-the-first-water sense. She was too real. Her eyes glittered brightly, her cheeks showed a delicate blush that owed nothing to artifice. His cousin was getting a prize, and Miles felt disconcerted by that thought.

He handed her back the bonnet in exchange for his sketchbook and they continued up to the terrace. Lady Oakley had retreated to the house when the wind kicked up, but she waited for them just inside the doors.

"Well done, Viscount Redinger. Well done. Quite knightly," she enthused.

Miles looked at her askance but couldn't prevent his lips from kicking up in a half smile. "It must be the atmosphere of my surroundings," he said smoothly. "I think I feel a poem coming on..."

Wide-eyed, Ann tried to suppress a giggle. She placed a hand across her lips to hide her laughter. He was earnest in playing Lord Redinger!

He threw his shoulders back and swaggered into the parlor. "Do you recall the last poem I sent to you?" he asked, affecting Redinger's manner.

"How could I forget the dew?" Ann exclaimed, looking everywhere except at him, for she feared she would burst into laughter.

Miles dropped his Redinger posture. "Now that is a part that would be best to forget," he said wryly.

Ann shrugged. "You asked."

"I did, indeed."

"What are you two nattering on about?" Lady Oakley demanded.

"The theatrical you scripted for us, my lady," Miles said. "Are we not merely players on your stage?"

Ann tucked her hair behind her ears and rocked on her toes as she listened to the Duke and Lady Oakley.

Lady Oakley stared at Miles. She tilted her head to the side. "I underestimated you, you are not who society believes you are, the reclusive, socially inept Duke. I shall need to remind myself—once again—not to give gossip credence. At my age, you'd think I'd have learned by now. I shall have to warn Vivian."

"But I am! It is Redinger who is not, and as I am he, I must rise above my inner desire to avoid others and be social." He made a face.

"You are wicked. You have turned our game on its head," she said with a laugh. "It will be interesting to see how this plays out with the Duchess, for she is the playwright, not I. I sought you out to tell you everyone is to meet in the grand parlor before dinner. We have pushed dinner back to seven due to late arrivals."

"Good, that will give me the opportunity to repair the wind damage," Ann said, pushing hair away from her face again.

"And perhaps don a gown without grass stains," Lady Oakley suggested, staring pointedly at the green stain along the hem of her muslin gown.

Ann laughed. "That as well!" She turned to Miles. "Thank you for the walk and conversation." She curtsied.

"The pleasure was mine," he answered, but she had already turned to run with a surprisingly light step out of the room. He looked over at Lady Oakley. "My cousin is a most fortunate gentleman in his bride."

"Perhaps," she said enigmatically.

"Tell me, Lady Oakley, how did you and the Duchess know I was with the Hallowells? This wasn't a spur-of-the-moment bit of mischief to call me Redinger. Did Mrs. Hallowell send a letter ahead?"

She laughed. "No, what she sent were her servants ahead of you. They informed the staff here, and the staff informed the Duchess."

"Ah, and in the moment, she decided I would be Redinger because Mrs. Hallowell gave her no forewarning."

"Precisely."

"So Redinger I will be for the nonce. Please excuse me, my lady, I, too, need to repair the effects of my time outside," he said, bowing over her hand.

"Of course, of course." She waved her hand dismissively.

Miles smiled and left the room. With Miss Hallowell for company, and the antics of the Duchess and Lady Oakley, this might prove to be an entertaining house party.

CHAPTER 7
THE GATHERING

The ice-blue dress her maid laid out disappointed Ann. The color shrieked an aloof character. Most evenings Ann enjoyed the aloof persona she donned like she would don a masquerade mask. It protected her from the worst of the fortune hunters. She was not wealthy, by any means; however, she would bring to her marriage an easy competence that many gentlemen would desire, if not for her scarred face.

She did not want to wear that aloof mask, at least not on the first night of the gathering.

"Lucy," she said. "I think I would prefer the rose gold dress tonight."

"But miss, it ain't been pressed yet," declared her horrified maid.

"How badly wrinkled can it be?"

"Bad, miss. That beautiful fabric shows every wrinkle. It is a dress fer standin' up in, not sittin'," declared Lucy.

"That is unfortunate! I can see the next time I go to the dressmaker, I need to bring you along to advise me on what fabrics are best."

"I only knows fabric based on what I been left to iron or clean."

"Are any of my other gowns in better shape that I could wear other than this ice-blue?"

"The cream and sage green gown, I should think. And you have that beautiful cream shawl with the heavy fringe that be shot with gold.

"All right. Bring that one out instead. We'll save the ice-blue for when I want an icy appearance," Ann said.

"As you say, miss," said Lucy. She gathered up the ice-blue dress and took it to the armoire in the corner of the room. She returned with a dress with an embroidered sage green bodice that had a pale cream net overdress embellished with swirls and rosettes along the hem over a sarsenet underdress.

"Yes, that will be fine," Ann said. "And you can thread the green and gold ribbon I bought last week through my hair."

"Yes, miss. That will look very well," Lucy said as she helped Ann remove the dress she'd worn outside.

"Grandmother wants everyone to meet downstairs in the grand parlor thirty minutes before dinner, likely for introductions all around before we sit together at dinner."

"That's what I been told when I was belowstairs. Said I should be gettin' upstairs to assist you for the greetin', as that Mrs. Weaver, the housekeeper, called it. I don't know if'n I should say this, Miss, but the staff all appear a bit jumpy, like scared rabbits. Oh, they be nice enough, but they be quietly remindin' each other not to talk too freely."

"Really?" Ann half turned toward her maid. "Are you certain you are not jumpy yourself being in a strange household?"

"No, miss. I remark on it as it is so odd against how

nice and friendly they be. Like that is how they would be, but somethin' has been happenin' that has them worriet, but they won't talk of it. Like it's some mystery."

"Mystery?" Ann considered that. "That would be like Grandmother to be planning something out of the ordinary by way of amusement."

"But why would somethin' her grace might be plannin' have her staff so distraught?"

"That is a good question," Ann said as she handed the ribbon to Lucy to weave through her hair. She watched her maid carefully place and pin the ribbon in place. "I think that works rather well," she said.

"Yes, miss, it be the perfect finish for your gown. Let me get your shawl and you'll be ready to join the others downstairs even before the deadline set by the Dowager Duchess."

Ann laughed. "Yes, mustn't be late. Better to be early!"

MILES CONSIDERED the clothing his valet had laid out for him for the evening. "William, do you think my cousin Sebastian would wear this?"

William Berryman snorted. "Hardly, Your Grace—I mean, my lord," he said, correcting himself.

"Yes, I agree. I am too staid compared to my cousin. Do I have anything that would come closer to what my cousin would wear?"

Berryman's brow furrowed as he considered the question. "The Viscount? No, except maybe the red-gold figured waistcoat," he tentatively suggested.

"Egad, man, you brought that? You know I never wear it." Miles saw a blush creep up the sides of his valet's neck and tinge his ears. "But you are correct, that is a waistcoat Sebastian would wear, so I will wear it tonight," he said with a grimace.

"Tonight, Your Gr— my lord?"

Miles nodded. "Tonight. The Dowager Duchess would have me be the Viscount Redinger so I shall dress and play the role. And you need to get better at addressing me as my lord."

His valet nodded slowly. "I—I heard below stairs that the Dowager Duchess is known in her family for the pranks she pulls on her children and grandchildren," he said hesitantly.

"I hear something else in your voice," Miles said. He crossed his arms over his chest.

"The staff are nervous, my lord; however, none will say why."

"Nervous how? What is your sense?"

Berryman scratched the bald spot on his head. "Like they are waiting for something to happen."

"Like the Dowager Duchess playing some roguery on her house guests?"

"Mayhap that is it. I can't say, Your Grace. Just, they're remote, like they are afraid to talk to any staff of the guests."

"I think you can relax, William, for the Dowager Duchess has already played her roguery on me by refusing to acknowledge who I am. She is insisting I am Viscount Redinger and has enlisted Lady Oakley in her declaration. I am not to argue it, but allow it to play out. Since my prank is defined, I can enjoy watching for what she has devised for the rest of the guests."

"I'm sure it is as you say, Your Grace," his man said with a weak laugh.

"Find that damned waistcoat and let me get down

to dinner and the next part of the Dowager Duchess's play."

~

WHEN THE FOOTMAN opened the doors to the grand parlor, the dim light in the room surprised Miles. It took him a moment to take in the scene before him. The Dowager Duchess sat in a winged chair near the fireplace, the flames sending dancing light on her rust-colored silk gown and the diamonds at her throat. Her companion, Mrs. Morrison, sat at the other side of the fireplace, a brown wren with bright, inquisitive eyes. Her fingers, threaded with yarn, worked long knitting needles. She scarcely heeded what she was doing, her eyes darting from person to person in the room. When their eyes met, she inclined her head in acknowledgement before sliding her glance away to the others in the room.

There were only five others present, besides the Duchess and her. Miles didn't know any of them.

"There you are, Redinger! Come in, come in!" the Dowager Duchess said, waving for him to come toward her.

He obliged and leaned over to kiss the back of her gloved hand. "Your Grace," he murmured, his eyes laughing though he kept a rein on his smile.

She smiled coquettishly at him and winked. He raised an eyebrow.

"I would make you known to my friends, Lord and Lady Thomas Druffner," she said, indicating the couple on a sofa set at right angles to her chair.

The lady nodded, but scarcely looked up from her needlepoint. The gentleman rose and extended two fingers. "Galborough's get?" he asked. "Known him and his lady twenty-odd years now. Met you when you was in short pants, you know."

"No, I didn't know," Miles said. If the gentleman did not perceive he was not a Galborough, he had not the association he claimed. Miles didn't hold it against him, though. If he really knew Galborough, he might not be as ready to claim acquaintance.

His uncle was a sour, dry stick. His opinions were truth and not to be questioned. On the day of the reading of Miles' late uncle's will that formally thrust him into the Ellinbourne dignities, Galborough had the temerity to order Miles to throw away all his paints and canvases now that he was a duke. His Countess quietly reminded her husband that Miles possessed a higher rank than his now and was not to be ordered. The Earl grumbled, and frowned, and stomped off to sit in a chair near the solicitor's desk. Thankfully, he hadn't seen his uncle since, though he did send periodic letters of *instruction*.

Sebastian did not take after his father, being more like his mother's Wingate side of the family.

"And here," the Duchess said, leading him to the corner of the room, "is Dr. Kurt Burkholdt from Germany, his wife, Frau Doktor Burkholdt, and his young associate Jacob—"

"Holbein, Your Grace," said the nervous young man beside Dr. Burkholdt. He glanced up at his mentor, then back at the Duchess.

"Yes, Holbein, like the Dutch artist," she said. "Jacob Holbein. I will contrive to remember, Herr Holbein," she said, patting his arm with her closed fan.

The young man stuttered something incomprehensible, bowed awkwardly and hurried back into the far recesses of the corner of the room he'd been in before Miles entered.

Miles exchanged greetings with Dr. Burkholdt and his wife.

"Dr. Burkholdt is an art history scholar and an expert on Michelangelo," the Duchess continued. "I have invited him to see my sketches to authenticate them, if he might."

Dr. Burkholdt bowed stiffly. "Ja, zough I have warned Her Grace zat many artists copy ze great Michelangelo to practice drawing. Zey do not mean to push zeir work as the great artist; however, zere are unscrupulous men who take advantage of zem, you know?"

"I can understand that," Miles said. It was all he could do to not admit that in his younger years he, too, copied the great artists to learn technique and style.

But that was Miles that did that, he'd reminded himself, not Viscount Redinger. Redinger had no desire to be an artist, just a poet, at least this week. No telling what his cousin's next obsession would be. Hopefully, it would be more apropos than writing bawdy poetry.

The Dowager Duchess smiled at the German scholar. "The Germans have developed the history of art as a scholarly pursuit. Dr. Burkholdt is in England to spread the philosophy of art history as worthy of academic inquiry."

"I applaud your efforts, sir," Miles said.

"You like ze art?" Dr. Burkholdt asked.

Miles looked down a moment to command his features to neutrality. When he looked up, he nodded politely at the gentleman. "Yes, I do."

Next to him, the Dowager Duchess smirked. He turned his head to look at her. Her smirk turned into a laugh. She covered her lips with a gloved hand.

"You wrote this script, not I," Miles reminded her.

"I had little notion how good you are at it!" she said.

Dr. Burkholdt looked between them, confused. *"Vas?"*

"My apologies, *Herr Doktor*," said the Duchess. She hooked her arm in his. "Let me introduce you to some art collectors who have just joined us," she said, leading him toward the door where two gentlemen were sizing each other up as if deciding if they should call their seconds. Frau Burkholdt trailed behind; her thin lips pursed together.

Miles recognized one of the gentlemen as Viscount Wolfred, a noted collector of questionable acquisition habits. The other gentleman he surmised to be a like-minded gentleman. Both men wore severe black. Wolfred a beady-eyed raven while his adversary was a fat black French Crèvecœur chicken, with a wild mane of black hair like the crest of the Crèvecœur cock. He could picture the two of them in a Thomas Rowlandson caricature.

Behind the bird-brained collectors he saw the Hallowell ladies and Colonel Brantley enter. He went forward to greet them.

"Finally, familiar faces," he said as he came up to them. He bowed over Mrs. Hallowell's hand and inclined his head to Ann. "I've never been comfortable in a crowd of strangers. Comes from growing up in the parsonage of a village, I suppose," he said with an easy smile.

"But didn't you go away to a school?" Ann asked.

"Yes, but not until I was twelve. My grandfather sent me to Eton. He thought I was spending too much time with my Uncle Clarence."

"But Clarence Wingate was a renowned artist!" protested Ann.

"Eventually, but not at the beginning. Uncle Clarence clawed his way to fame as most artists of any sort do."

"Have you had to do that?" she asked.

"I did and being Clarence Wingate's nephew has not helped. I had to ensure my style is far removed from his. But now?" He shrugged with a wry smile. "I don't quite know what I am."

"No! Don't say so!" Ann protested, louder than she intended. To her chagrin, the low babble of conversation in the room halted for a moment. She looked around, embarrassed, then raised her fingers to her lips and giggled softly.

Miles was entranced. Damn his cousin. "Have you any knowledge of why your grandmother has kept this room so dark?" he asked, changing the subject to something less sensitive to himself. "I wonder how either Lady Druffner or Mrs. Morrison can see what they are about in this light."

Ann nodded, schooling her face to seriousness. "No. And I can't see how it might encourage guests to mingle. One would be afraid of tripping on a chair leg in the dark or some such thing."

"Precisely my thought."

"I believe there is a tinderbox on that table by the window. Shall we?"

"I say artists need light to see their world whether they are in the throes of creation or not."

Miles followed Ann across the room, stopping only to grab a branch of unlit candles from the table next to Mrs. Morrison.

Ann opened the tinder box, taking out the flint and striker. "Would you do the honors, Your Grace?"

"My lady, you are confusing me with another. It must be this damnable light. Standing before you is a viscount." He flourished a bow, then took the items from her.

"I believe you are enjoying the viscount role," Ann observed. "You are not nearly as formal as you were when we met."

Miles considered that. "I believe you are correct. The eight gold strawberry leaves had become quite weighty." He lit the first candle, then used it to light the others on the branch he'd brought over and the branch on the table. "I shall return this branch next to the table by Mrs. Morrison."

"Excellent idea. I shall put this one next to Lady Druffner. Do you think my grandmother will notice?"

He looked across the room at the Dowager Duchess. "If she does, she won't say anything. But I don't think her butler will like it. We may need to protect the light. Lamentably, I have neither sword nor pistol about my person."

"Me neither," Ann said, mimicking his serious mien. "But I am prepared to sally forth."

"Then sally we shall," Miles said, picking up the candle branch.

He carried it over to Mrs. Morrison and carefully placed it on the table to cast the best light on her work.

She looked up, startled. He winked at her. She smiled and resumed her knitting.

Ann picked up the other branch of candles, surprised at the hefty weight. She placed her other hand underneath the base to support the weight as she walked over to Lady Druffner. Sliding behind Lord Druffner, she set the candles on the table and pushed it toward Lady Druffner.

Lady Druffner lifted her head and blinked owlishly.

"This should help you," Ann told her, lightly touching her forearm.

"Oh, yes, yes. I believe it shall. Thank you, my dear," Lady Druffner said.

Ann smiled reassurance, then looked up to where her grandmother stood. As Miles predicted, her grandmother didn't seem to notice or care about the light.

At that moment, the door to the parlor opened to admit Lady Oakley on the arm of Ann's favorite uncle, Aidan Nowlton. Ann knew Aidan was one person who could spoil the play, for he assuredly would know the Duke of Ellinbourne! She hurried toward the door.

"Did you warn him?" she asked Lady Oakley.

"No, not yet. We just came across each other in the hall."

"Warn me about what?" Aidan asked languidly. "Is my mother indulging in mischief again?" He pursed his lips against a wry, lazy smile.

"Yes."

He sighed. "What are we to endure? Breakfast for dinner?"

"Nothing so simple. And besides, she has done that before," Ann said. "You know she doesn't repeat her pranks. See the gentleman talking with Colonel Brantley and my stepmother?"

"You mean Ell—"

Ann pressed the tips of her fingers against his lips. "No, that is not who you think it to be. At least, not to Grandmama. She is calling him Redinger."

"Viscount Redinger?"

"Yes."

"But isn't that who she has picked for your husband?"

Ann half-smiled and shrugged. "I have to marry someone."

"Poppycock!" Lady Oakley said. "And so I told Vivian when she told me the plan. Ridiculous! She hasn't seen Redinger since he was in short pants."

Aidan smirked. "I'd have to agree with Lady Oakley. Not right for you."

"But I need to marry so Ursula will accept Colonel Brantley's suit. She feels it is her duty as my stepmother, to see to my future before herself, which I grant you is ridiculous. But that does beg the question, where should I live? I don't want to go live with her and Brantley, even if he is a dear."

"What about living with Arthur and. his family? You know they would welcome you." Aidan suggested.

Ann looked at him severely. "Could you live in an homage to Arthurian legends?"

Lady Oakley snorted. "She makes a good argument, Aidan."

Aidan sighed. "I see I shall have to give this consideration. But under no circumstances are you to accept a suit from Redinger, and I'm certain my brother, as head of the family, would agree."

He looked across the room to see Ellinbourne approaching. "But your pseudo Redinger is another matter," he mused, tapping a long, graceful finger against his lips.

Ann looked at him, horrified. "Stop it! I know how you are, Aidan Nowlton! Do not think to manipulate him in such a fashion."

"Moi?"

Ann glared at him. Beside her, Lady Oakley giggled. That made Ann laugh. There was something about an older woman giggling that highlighted the ridiculousness of their conversation.

Miles approached them, smiling. "This looks like a dangerous group."

Aidan raised an eyebrow, his smile slow. "Well met, Redinger," he said archly.

Miles inclined his head.

The butler came in the double doors, frowned at the candles by Lady Druffner and Amanda, then announced dinner. He pulled a candle snifter from his pocket as the guests passed him, walking to the dining room.

Miles extended his arm to Ann.

Ann hooked her arm through his. At the door, Miles casually took the candle snifter from the butler's hand. "The ladies need light for their art. Do not deprive them," he said.

The butler blanched, "I wasn't, but Her Grace—"

Miles held up a hand to stop the man's excuses.

"Very ducal," Ann whispered as they passed out of the room.

Miles looked down at her and frowned, his mouth twisting wryly. "And totally unlike my cousin. I don't know for how long I will be able to keep up this play."

"Grandmama will probably grow tired of it tomorrow, especially since you have so easily assumed the role she gave you. I warn you; she may try to disconcert you by addressing you as the Duke of Ellinbourne tomorrow and act like that was always the case."

"Thank you for the warning. I shall prepare for the jump."

Ann's eyes sparkled with mirth. "This is amazingly fun."

At the entrance to the dining room, Miles was dismayed to discover he was not seated next to Ann. Instead, he was seated across from her. In between them sat a large wrought silver epergne in the Chinese style with snarling dragons holding small crystal bowls of salt and pepper, Buddhist monks in various activities surrounded the large central crystal bowl, and a Phoenix rose from the central bowl's silver lid.

The shy Lady Druffner sat to his right and the sour Frau Burkholdt sat to his left.

Miles inhaled deeply and slowly let his breath out. It would be a dreary meal.

CHAPTER 8

THE RAVEN AND THE FRENCH
CHICKEN

Ann pushed the heavy pink and green striped bedroom drapes aside to allow the morning sunlight to bathe her bedroom in that mystical early morning glow that bathed the landscape before the sun burned away the nighttime mists. She saw a gardener in the cutting garden filling a large wicker basket with fresh flowers for the vases of bouquets her grandmother liked to have displayed about the house. He moved methodically from one area to another, gathering the bright blossoms and deep greenery the housekeeper would use to add spring to rooms in the house. The gardener took care not to take too many flowers from any one spot, thereby ensuring the garden remained a joy for an afternoon stroll.

The garden was a changing palette of color nearly year-round owing to the glass house tucked up against one wall of the old monastery where the gardening staff cultivated flower and vegetable seedlings and grew fresh fruit trees and plants.

Well known for its parklands, Versely's head gardener hosted tours on Wednesdays in the summer for those wanting to take a closer look at the external wonders of the estate. The pennies charged for admission made their way to the village church's poor box.

Ann wondered what her grandmother's plans were for her museum. She could not see her grandmother collecting money from the curious who would come to see the artwork or just to satisfy their curiosity as to how the other half lived. She supposed she could hire a tour operator. Or maybe her grandmother would allow her to act as tour guide, Ann mused, smiling.

Though probably not. Her grandmother seemed too set on marrying her off. Her solicitor was due to arrive today, ostensibly to join the house party with his family; however, Ann knew he and grandmother would also discuss marriage settlements.

Ann screwed up her nose at that thought.

She was glad Viscount Redinger had not come.

She had convinced herself that she could go through with a marriage of convenience, that such an arrangement made a fine choice. It wasn't like she was a young miss in her first season, for circumstances had kept her out of society during her prime coming-out years. And did it matter who she married? Love matches seemed the exception rather than the rule, her parents being the exception. She knew her father's subsequent marriage to Ursula had been for the convenience of both, and she believed they'd had a good marriage until her father died. Shouldn't that be what she desired for herself? Especially with her facial scar? With its ugly jagged white line, it was worse than pox scars.

She sighed and started to turn away from the window when she spotted someone else outside. It was the Duke of Ellinbourne. He wore a slouch hat on his head and his overall attire spoke of disregard for his title. She smiled. His clothing reminded her of her favorite gray dress she liked to wear outdoors when she painted. He'd been painting. He carried an easel and canvas, along with a leather bag slung over his shoulder. She wondered what he would have painted this early. The morning mist? She wished she could see the canvas clearly.

She put her hand on the glass as she leaned closer to the window, trying to catch a glimpse. Ellinbourne looked up and saw her.

Ann gasped and jumped back from the window, for she was wearing her night rail without her wrapper. She felt warmth on her cheeks.

Gracious! She wasn't some young debutante just out of the schoolroom. There was no reason for being missish. They were some distance apart, and the windows wanted cleaning, she decided.

She turned when she heard the bedroom door latch click. Lucy pushed the door open with her hip as she balanced carrying in a tray.

"Coo, Miss Ann. What you be doin', up and standin' by the window?" She set the tray on a table near the fireplace. "I brung you some hot chocolate. 'Tis a bit brisk outside this mornin', though it look like it's to be a glorious day." She picked up Ann's pale blue wrapper from the end of the bed and held it out for her.

"Has grandmother decided on the activities for the day?" Ann asked as she slipped her arms into the wrapper and tied it closed.

"Yes, miss, and the staff have been instructed to rouse the guests and their servants to ensure everyone is downstairs and finished their breakfast for the art tour at ten."

"At ten? But I didn't think all the guests are here yet."

"No, miss, that they aren't. Her Grace has decided she would rather do smaller group tours."

"Coming from grandmother, that sounds suspicious. I wonder if she will be telling each group different information. She'd be delighted to see how long it would take each group to figure out the discrepancies."

Lucy frowned. "Would she truly do that?"

"Oh, yes. That is just the sort of thing she would do. The Duchess, for all her lofty title, loves a good laugh."

"Well, I say you can't fault a body for laughter." Lucy walked toward the armoire in the corner of the room. "I'd not the time to press all your dresses last evenin', but your green figured muslin and the blue on cream printed cotton have been pressed."

"I'll wear the printed cotton. That muslin can be a bit drafty, as fine as it is," Ann said. She sipped her hot chocolate.

"Yes, miss. I'm sorry I didna think of that yesterday when I took the dresses to press. I confess the muslin is easy to press, and the iron does not need to be that hot to do so."

Ann laughed. "I understand convenience. But for day I should like my cottons."

"Yes, miss."

"Lucy?" Ann said as she sat before the dressing table. She freed her hair from its nighttime braid and picked up her brush.

"Yes, miss?" Lucy asked, her voice muffled from inside the armoire.

"Were any of the guests up and about this morning when you came upstairs?

"Not that I saw, miss," Lucy said as she brought out the cream cotton gown with the roller printed blue decorative motif, a clean shift, corset, and stockings. "Though Lewis said the duke went out 'afore first light carryin' a large bag, a canvas and an easel. He thought it a mite suspicious seein' as how all manner of peculiar things be happenin'"

Ann stopped brushing her hair. She looked over at Lucy. "Who's Lewis and what did he mean by peculiar?"

"Lewis is the head footman."

"Head footman?"

"Yes, miss, like a butler in trainin' as how Mr. Botsford wants to retire next year."

"How odd, but I suppose reasonable given grandmother's plans. But what did he mean by peculiar?"

Lucy shook her head. "I don't know, miss. I didna think to ask."

Ann saw a faint blush creep up Lucy's neck. "Ah, that attractive, is he?"

Lucy's blush deepened. "As if I would step out with your grandmother's staff. Not likely. But he does have wavy blond hair with one curl that falls across his forehead," she said, a distant look in her eyes.

"Gracious! I see that I shall have to meet this paragon," Ann said with a laugh, "and perhaps discover what he means by 'peculiar'."

～

MILES CLIMBED the stairs to his suite, thoroughly disgusted with himself. He'd gone out early to paint the early morning fog, something he'd done many times on his estate. He knew the techniques for the transient effects of fog. Fog demanded a light hand, a dry brush, and small brush strokes. Today his hand was too heavy, there was too much paint on his brush, and his brush strokes were anything but small.

He knew what the problem was. This ridiculous play the Dowager Duchess had him act. And to what purpose? He laughed to himself as he laid the canvas down on the desk in this private parlor and dumped his bag on the floor.

Truth. It had been amusing to take on the mantle of his ne'er-do-well cousin. However, after a night's sleep, he wondered what he'd gotten himself into. That wasn't his style of behavior, especially since taking on the ducal coronet. Being a duke demanded a certain level of seriousness and decorum. The fortunes and lives—whole villages even—depended on him as their duke. And here he was playing a May game.

He should never have agreed to come to the house party.

He slouched down in the chair by the desk and ran a hand through his hair.

Truth again. Miss Hallowell's reaction to his cousin's bawdy poem drew him to her. How many young women would laugh after their initial shock and light-heartedly declare, *At least it rhymed*?

She was his cousin's intended, though Miles did not think they would suit. That was not for him to say, and certainly not for him to poach upon!

Brooding about his situation had impacted his art. He couldn't concentrate on what he was doing, his mind wandering. Typically, painting was a form of meditation. Not on this day.

It could be agony to continue to act as Redinger

and court Miss Hallowell, for who was he courting her
for? His cousin? Or himself? He was on the road to
heartache and didn't see any way to choose another
path.

He sighed and stood up. He pulled his kerchief
from around his neck and walked to the door of the
bedchamber. He couldn't hide now. Time to get ready
for the day. He wondered what William had set out for
him this morning.

WILLIAM TOLD Miles of the Duchess's plans for the
day, so Miles didn't have time to protest on the
clothing William set up for him: a blue superfine
jacket, buff pantaloons, a Pomona green and gold
striped waistcoat with a roguish black cravat. The
artist in him cringed at the combination; however,
there was no time to press any other attire pieces.

Miles glowered at his valet, for he supposed that
was William's intent. The man's taste sometimes lay
only in his mouth. He was good at keeping his
clothing cleaned, his boots polished, and his bar-
bering immaculate.

He stopped for a moment at the entrance to the
dining room. Owing to the size of the party, they
would use the large dining room for all meals. He understood that. What he did not understand, nor countenance, was the large epergne still in the center of the
table. The footman he'd seen when he'd left the
house now stood just inside the door. Miles turned
to him.

"Would you be so kind as to remove that?" he said,
pointing to the centerpiece.

"My lord?"

Miles waved his hand. "It is not conducive to casual conversation. Rather off-putting."

The footman bowed slightly and went to take the epergne from the table.

"Maybe you can find a closet to hide it in," Miles suggested.

The footman turned, a grin tugging at his lips.

"I heard that," Ann said, coming up behind Miles. "You must be Lewis," she said to the footman.

"Yes, miss." The footman inclined his head while trying to get a good hold on the awkward, ugly silver piece.

"Well, I agree on the suggested disposition," she said in a whisper. "See what you can do."

The footman's grin grew broader. "Certainly." In as stately a manner as he could contrive with the large piece in his arms, the footman left the dining room.

Miles extended his arm to Ann to lead her to a place at the table. "Thank you for your support. I'm sure the piece is valuable, but not good for the digestion. At least not mine."

Ann laughed. "Or that of many people! I thank you for the initiative you took."

"A bit high and mighty," he said ruefully. "Sometimes I think I've become too accustomed to the arrogance of being a duke."

"I think that was more the artist than the duke who decided the piece needed to go," she suggested.

"Ah, but the artist would have suffered in silence," he said as he drew out a chair for her.

"Then I am glad for the duke," she said, sliding gracefully into the chair.

"What duke?" demanded Lord Druffner.

"We were just discussing my cousin, the Duke of Ellinbourne," Miles said.

"So is traveling about the country living off of the benefices of friends and relatives while you lease out your own property," returned Nowlton with a sweet smile. "But have another cup of coffee," he suggested, smiling, signaling the footman to refill Lord Druffner's cup.

Ann and Miles exchanged glances.

"As to what this is all about, I am as at sea as you. The Duchess has forever been unique. Age has not changed her one whit," continued Nowlton as he languidly took a seat at the table.

"Nor shall it," added Ann.

Nowlton inclined his head in Ann's direction. "As you say, my dear niece, nor shall it."

The blond footman who'd taken away the epergne pulled the double doors open wide to admit the Duchess and Lady Oakley. The Dowager Duchess stood as regal as the Queen, her head up, her eyes tilted down, lips pursed, and her hands clasped in front of her, resting on the intricate gold embroidered vines running in wavy lines up her brown silk gown.

On seeing her, the gentlemen rose.

She looked over her assemblage of guests in the dining room, then she clapped her hands several times.

"Finish up now," she said loftily. "I gave you plenty of time. We shall meet in ten minutes in the grand hall to begin the tour. There is much to see and discuss. I am looking forward to your thoughts and ideas regarding my museum plans."

"Your Grace," began Lord Wolfred.

She ignored him and instead turned and left the dining room as grandly as she'd entered, Lady Oakley paused a moment to wink at Ann and Miles before she turned to follow the Duchess, and the footman solemnly closed the tall double doors after them.

Lord Wolfred angrily frowned, his brows drawing together as he slammed back down into his chair.

"Temper, temper," Nowlton admonished the art collector.

Ann laughed behind her napkin.

～

TEN MINUTES LATER, the extant house party guests dutifully gathered in the old armory hall—the entry to the manor in centuries past—awaiting their hostess. It was a cold and drafty gray stone room filled with arms and armor. The only color to enliven the space were the pennants and banners hanging from the dark oak ceiling beams and along the walls. Not even one of the gardener's bouquets of flowers was present to relieve the austere room.

After waiting an additional ten minutes, the blond footman opened the heavy carved oak doors to admit Lady Oakley.

"I'm afraid there has been a change of plans," she said, and by her demeanor, it was clear to Ann she wasn't happy about the change.

"There has been a late arrival, a party expected yesterday just arrived. They say they had carriage issues. The Duchess is seeing to their welcome and care."

"So are we to have this demmed tour or not?" Lord Druffner asked. "This is a demmed uncomfortable room to wait in, and not a chair about to sit in either."

Lady Oakley quirked one mobile eyebrow upward as she stared at him over her glasses. "Well, yes, I can see that. The Duchess has asked me to tell you the tour will be postponed until eleven o'clock as the Peverleys begged her Grace to join the tour and just grant them a bit of time to refresh themselves from the horrors of their travel—their words, not mine."

"Peverleys you say?" said Sir Robert. "Is that the Marquis of Peverley?"

Lady Oakley nodded. "It is."

"I won't get the time for a word with the Duchess with them here. They will monopolize her," grumbled Lord Wolfred.

"They'll wear her down until she practically gives the sketches to them," complained Sir Robert.

"What are you talking about?" Ann asked.

"Yes, I should like to know, too," said Nowlton.

"The Michelangelo sketches."

"What about them?" asked Nowlton.

"That's what I've come to purchase from her," said Lord Wolfred.

"You!" Sir Robert said. "I intend to have them."

"Nein," said Dr. Burkholdt. "Zay belong in a museum vhere they may be studied. I vould take zem back to Germany."

Miles crossed his arms over his chest. "Has it occurred to any of you that the Duchess may not wish to sell the sketches?" he asked.

Nowlton nodded. "I know that is not her intent. You are naïve if you believe you can come here and wave the flimsies in front of my mother's face and she'll turn the sketches over to you."

"Nein, you are but her child. She not convide in you. To vinance her plans she vill sell," Doktor Burkholdt said with confidence.

Sir Robert shouldered his way past Ann to come up to Burkholdt. Miles caught her as she fell back.

"And I can offer her the best price," said Sir Robert loftily, oblivious to his actions.

"Have a care, man," said Nowlton. "You nearly knocked over my niece."

Sir Robert ignored him. He looked down on Doktor Burkholdt who stood a good half a foot shorter. The men glared at each other.

A shrill whistle shattered the tension in the room.

Everyone turned to the source. It was Lady Oakley, with two fingers at her lips. She lowered her hands and grinned. "Haven't done that in nigh on fifty years. Didn't know if I still could," she said delightedly. "Now, if we could have done with the fighting cocks, I would appreciate it. There are more refreshments in the dining room, should you need anything else to eat or drink while we are waiting."

She turned to leave then stopped and looked back at the group. "I should tell you that Lewis, here," she said, pointing at the footman, "has instructions to remove anyone from the Duchess's presence who pesters her too much. And he has the authority to decide what is pestering and what is not, regardless of rank."

The footman, standing by the open door, smiled wolfishly and bowed to the company as Lady Oakley left the room. He extended his arm to invite everyone to leave as well.

"Uncle Aidan," Ann said, staying her uncle when he would have left the room with the others. "Stay a moment." A troubled expression pinched her cheeks. "You too," she said to Miles.

"Oh, don't call me Uncle. It makes me feel too old," complained Nowlton with mock dismay.

Ann smiled slightly. "Be serious. I don't understand

what is going on, but grandmother is up to something. I'm worried," she said.

"I know this house party was to have two purposes. One being an opportunity for Viscount Redinger and I to consider a match. To my understanding, the second was to allow others to see her art collection and discuss turning what is left of the old monastery into an art gallery museum."

"That is true," Nowlton said. "But what you don't understand is the art world can be cutthroat. Those who mother has invited is reasonable for her goals, the best of the best; however, as with the best, so goes the jealousy and games. Do not refine too much on the antipathy between the principals. I find it quite entertaining. Note I did not take offense to our German guest's belittling comment. That is part of their game."

"If you say so," Ann said slowly.

"I do," her uncle assured her. "Now, let's join the guests. I could use another cup of coffee." Nowlton followed after the others.

Miles looked down at Ann. "You continue to have doubts."

"Yes," she said. "I spent time with grandmother when we were cataloging Lady Travis's collection. She does not take art collecting as a pastime, just as you don't take painting as a pleasant pastime, whereas I do. The intent is different and therefore the thoughts and emotions tied up with it are different. There is a purpose for Herr Doktor Burkholdt, the two collectors, and the Peverleys being here. They all have a streak of something that makes me uncomfortable. If the party was for her art gallery museum, then why not include those who are on the board of the Royal Academy of Art?"

"It is the beginning of the season," Miles reminded her.

"I know; however, I still think one or two would have come. I wonder if any of them were invited? Mrs. Morrison would know. I will ask her."

"Since we have some time available and I know I do not wish to be around the rest of the house party right now, why don't we indulge in our favored pastime?"

"Painting?"

"I was thinking more in terms of sketching."

Ann laughed. "Sketch with you? I am not in your league. I should be embarrassed."

"A musician practices odd bits and pieces. They don't always play complete compositions. They repeat passages they are not happy with; they practice scales to improve their hand and brain coordination, they do not always produce beautiful sounds. Art is no different. I sketch to maintain my eye and hand coordination, I work on perspective, light and shadow, and mood."

"Mood?"

"Yes. Take a vase or a statue to draw. Do one sketch rendering a dark, dramatic emotion. Do a second of the same item, rendering a light, comedic emotion."

"I don't know how one would do that."

"Would you like to learn?"

"Yes, I would!"

"In the parlor we were in last night, remember the porcelain statue on the table where you found the tinder box?"

"Yes, that is one of my aunt's pieces from her Shakespeare's Sonnets collection."

"Your aunt?"

"Elizabeth Nowlton Littledean. She is a sculptress.

That particular piece is how she came to meet and marry Josiah Littledean."

"Of Littledean Fine Porcelain?"

"The same. I understand it was a great scandal at the time, but grandmother supported her."

"Good for her. Then we should definitely sketch that piece. Let's fetch our sketching supplies and meet there."

"All right. I am looking forward to this notion of sketching mood," Ann said as they left the library.

CHAPTER 9
THE STATUE

"It's not here!" Ann set her sketch portfolio on a nearby chair and walked over to the table where the statue stood the previous night. She ran her fingers across the top of the table as if to magically make the statue appear again.

"They probably moved it to another location," Miles said. He set his portfolio down next to Ann's.

"It's stood here for as long as I can remember," she said quietly. She looked about the room, at all the surfaces available for statuary. It was not in the room.

"The footman who moved that table centerpiece monstrosity is stationed in the entrance hall. Perhaps he moved it," Miles suggested.

Ann nodded. "Good thought." She swept past Miles and walked back out into the hall.

"Lewis!" she called.

The footman straightened and looked toward her. "Yes, miss? Is there something you require?"

She walked toward him. "In the parlor, on the table by the oriel window, was a porcelain statue of two young lovers. It's not there now. Did you move it?"

"No, miss. You say it is not there?"

"Yes, it is not there, and I know it was last night."

The footman nodded. A frown creased his forehead. "Objects have been disappearing for several hours or a day," he confessed. "Has been happening all week. But it turns up eventually in a different location, not where they belong."

"What kind of objects?"

"Art objects. Paintings, drawings, sculptures—any of the art pieces that are easily moved are being moved. The staff is concerned."

Ann laughed. "If they do turn back up and are just in a different place than I would guess, this is another of Grandmother's pranks."

The footman frowned. "I should hope not, miss. With all that is going on, that would be most unfortunate and make things difficult."

"Difficult?" Ann asked.

The footman seemed to shake off whatever he had been thinking. He smiled down on Ann. "Nothing, miss," he said affably.

Ann looked doubtfully at him. "Well, thank you for that information," she said as she turned to walk back to the parlor where Miles stood at the doorway.

"What is it?" he asked.

"He said objects have been disappearing all week, then reappearing later in a different location. That has had the servants jumpy."

"One of your grandmother's pranks to see if people notice?" Miles said.

"That is what I suggested to the footman, and he said something about he hoped that was not the case as that would make it more difficult. When I pressed him about his use of the word 'difficult' he said 'nothing' and resumed a smiling expression when moments before he looked perturbed."

"Hmm. That is odd."

"I'll ask Lady Oakley about this. She and Grandmother seem to be quite of a mind."

"Probably a good idea. Shall we find another item to sketch or wait?"

"Wait. I think it is nearly time and I hear others coming now."

They walked out into the hall.

A tall woman in a deep rose-colored gown was descending the stairs. Behind her came a portly gentleman with a frizzy brown fringe of hair around his head. Ann assumed these were the Peverleys. There was a decided air of privilege about the couple. They scarcely looked anywhere except their hostess, who stood at the base of the stairs awaiting them.

Lord Wolfred was again trying to engage the Duchess in conversation.

"Not now, Lord Wolfred," the Duchess said kindly. She smiled at the man, though she ignored his importuning. Ann saw her look up at the footman and nod slightly. The blond footman came to her side, steering Lord Wolfred away by the simple expedient of standing between them as he leaned forward to hear what the Duchess said.

"Are we all here, now?" the Duchess asked. She looked about the group. "I was intending to start in the armory; however, seeing as how you spent a long time in there this morning, we will skip that room. If anyone has any questions about the items in that room, we can discuss them later. Right now, I'd like to talk to you about the paintings along the stairway. You have all had an opportunity to see them on your way to and from your rooms but let me tell you some interesting facts about the artists who created the portraits lining the stairs and in the halls."

She led the party up the grand staircase, talking continually about the artists and the people whose pictures stared down at them.

"These are, of course, the Malmsby family portraits. They go five back five hundred years. The first duke had them brought here in 1662 when he was granted the property by the crown after the death of the last Versely. He decided this would be the new family seat. Good thing he did, for it wasn't a month afterward that there was a fire at Malmsby Castle on the coast that destroyed everything inside."

"Down this hall to the left is the long gallery. The third Duke had it remodeled just to hang art pieces. My favorite landscapes are there—at least what I could fit in the room and remain out of direct sunlight. It is nearly as crammed with paintings as a Royal Academy of Art spring show."

She paused as everyone looked around at the long room. The gallery had three fireplaces, one on each of the end walls and one in the middle of the inside wall. The four oriel windows let in light; however, the roofs of each had an overhang which prevented the hottest and brightest light of the day from shining into the room. The patina of the old wood linenfold paneling provided a warm backdrop for the framed art hung from hooks on the picture railing.

"I do not like everything jumbled together in this way. There is no place to rest the eye to give yourself a space for reflection. Note the small windows at the ceiling? They do not let in direct sunlight; however, they allow filtered light to bathe the room in daylight. Actually, when the moon is full, the room has a lovely glow. Bertram and I used to sit here in the evening, drinking our cordials and listening to the silence."

"But now, let's look at the old monastery wing.

There is not much in this area yet as there is much building repair that needs to be done. However, it is a stunning area for its carved wood ornamentation and its priest holes and tunnels."

"Priest holes?" parroted Lord Wolfred, his eyebrows rising high on his forehead.

"Oh, my, yes. They are the reason Malmsby wanted the property. Rumor had it that the monks had a fortune hidden on the property. Malmsby paid a high price to the king for the chance to find the treasure of the monks."

"Was it ever found?"

The Duchess laughed. "No, there was no great treasure. There seldom is, but the hunt is what people enjoy, I think. There were some pieces of interest found, like ecclesiastical items and the epergne in the dining room," the Duchess said casually, avoiding mention of later discoveries.

Miles and Ann glanced at each other at the mention of the epergne.

"The entrance to the old monastery is through a door in this hall. Do you think you could find it?"

"A hidden door?" Lord Druffner asked.

"Yes, a hidden door." Her smile hovered on a smirk.

All the company began to look.

Herr Burkholdt directed his assistant where to knock on the wood as he listened for echoes. The Raven and the French Chicken chose the same area to investigate and glared at each other as they worked sections of the wall. The Druffners chose the corner to investigate.

"Aren't you going to join the search?" Ann asked Miles.

"When I know you are aware of this hidden door? No. I would just embarrass myself with my efforts."

"But it's part of the fun!"

"Notice the Peverleys are not looking either," he said by way of defense. They were sitting on a sofa facing the fireplace looking ineffably bored.

Miles stood back and looked at the walls and the artwork. "Ah, I see one of my uncle's paintings," he said with a smile. "I remember him working on that one."

"I told you Grandmother had one of his paintings," Ann said, walking up to stand beside him to survey the room.

He studied the picture for a moment, remembering his uncle's commentary as he painted. Then he frowned. "Wait a moment." He looked intently at that picture, then at two other paintings in the room that were of a similar size. "It is affixed to the wall, not hung from the picture railing," he mused.

He saw Ann compress her lips tightly against smiling and duck her head to hide her expression. But was what he suspected the truth?

He walked over to the painting and studied the frame and the area around the picture, then he walked over to each of the other two paintings and studied them.

He turned to the Duchess. "Your Grace, there is not one entrance to the monastery from this room. There are three."

"Yes!" Ann cried gleefully, clapping her hands together.

"Ann! Calm yourself," her grandmother reprimanded with an indulgent smile.

"What? What?" cried Lord Druffner from where he knelt on one knee on the floor, tapping the base boards. He hand-walked his way up the wall. "What's this? Three entrances? Impossible."

"The Viscount is correct," the Duchess announced to everyone. "There are three entrances to the old monastery from this room." She turned to Miles. "Do you know how to open the entrances?"

"Possibly," he said. He walked back to his uncle's picture and ran his hand over the frame. It was an old-fashioned ornate frame, not at all suitable for the picture within it. His fingers felt a piece high on the side move slightly. He looked closer. There, where one piece of framing joined another was a small lever. He pushed it up and heard a click. He pushed slightly on the wall and it swung silently inward on well-oiled hinges.

He looked back at the assembled company. "I believe this is the next stop on our tour."

Lord Druffner shouldered him aside to see the picture frame and its hidden lever. "*Hmph*, demme," he muttered.

Miles retreated back into the long gallery. "Good work Your Gr—my lord," Ursula enthused.

"We could have used you in the Home Office," Colonel Brantley said.

"To work for my uncle?" Ann asked. "No, and no, and no. I wouldn't want that for anyone."

"Why is that?" Miles asked.

"Remember when I told you I'd seen that other painting by your uncle? We were only there because we could be of use to him as a cover for his activities."

"Miss Hallowell, you mustn't say such things," remonstrated Colonel Brantley. "The man is a hero."

"Standing on the graves of others," she said softly.

"Now, now, Miss Hallowell."

"It is over now, anyway. He is no longer in his position," Ursula interjected hastily.

"Yes." Brantley rocked back on his heels. "Retired last year," he said, then shut his lips tight against saying anything else.

"He's settled at Malvern Hall, his ancestral home. It's not over five miles away. That made my aunt happy to get away from London and be back in the area," Ann said over her shoulder as she walked toward the monastery door. She saw Miles's curiosity and was thankful he didn't ask more questions.

Lord Candelstone was a hero to some and a villain to others. She had heard someone blackmailed her uncle into retirement. By Colonel Brantley's reaction, he knew it too. Lord Candelstone was one of those ardent loyalists to King and country who thought any means to achieve an end justified—even the lives of his countrymen and women.

Ursula, Miles, and Colonel Brantley followed her.

Inside they saw the others peering into the small monks's rooms, pulling open cupboards and tapping walls. None of them taking the time to see the monastery for its beauty.

All the monks's doors were heavy oak with intricate carving of biblical derived images. The stone walls had at one time been whitewashed. Crosses of varied material and design hung on the walls between the small rooms. One room was bigger than the rest and had its own fireplace.

"The Abbot's room, I presume," said Miles.

"Yes. As children, my cousins and I played hide and seek here." She smiled. "Lancelot, he was the oldest and the tallest. There were some spaces he could not get into that others of us could. He would good-naturedly grumble when he was 'it'."

"It sounds like you had a good childhood."

She considered that. "I did, for the most part. I was an only child and since father was in the diplomatic service, he and mother spent most of the time in other countries. If I wasn't visiting one relation or another, I was at Mrs. Lansbury's Academy for Young Women.

"Grandmother often said I could just live with her and have a governess; however, my father insisted I have a proper education that included the sciences and math. I am not proficient in any of the 'lady arts' except for drawing, as we had drawing classes to support our science and architecture studies."

"Architecture?"

She nodded. "Part of the math curriculum."

"Ah."

She laughed. "It was because of that training I was able to find a couple more hidden rooms in the monastery that no one had found in the past one hundred years. I was drawing floor plans of the area for fun and noticed some oddities which led me to more hidden areas."

She pointed down to the floor. "For example, there is a four-foot space between the Abbot's room floor and the ceiling of the room below."

"What did you find there?"

"Richly decorated vestments and banners, heavy chains, incense burners, a finger bone in a blue velvet-lined box, treasures, yes, but Church treasures, not the gold and jewels people hope to find when they speak of treasure."

"A finger bone?"

"Yes, from what we have been able to learn it was the finger bone of one of the saints. It was a valuable relic. The archbishop has it now, along with all the other church related items. Though they were

Catholic in nature, the Church of England did not hesitate to take the items."

"I would think not. Probably still of great value."

"Yes, and a gold crucifix is still gold and still a crucifix. Just needed a new sprinkling of holy water to become an Anglican icon."

He laughed.

"Seriously, what I think was the most important find was a series of stained-glass-windows. Six in all. The colors are unbelievable. Grandmother intends to have them restored. Those will be the last items done. I can't wait to see the color stream into the main gathering room below from those windows."

"They weren't chapel windows?"

"We don't think so. But the original chapel burned down during the Reformation and the windows on the ground floor are the right size. Doesn't matter. I just know the orientation of that room will show the windows to the best effect."

"All that architectural training."

She laughed. "Perhaps."

"Come, everyone," called out the Duchess. "We have dallied here long enough. Next is the porcelain room and then the green parlor, where I have all my sketches and prints. That is my favorite room, so of course I save it to last."

"Porcelain room? Bah, why don't we go the sketch room now. That's what we all want to see, anyway," said Lord Druffner.

"Patience, Lord Druffner, all in good time," said the Duchess.

She swept around and went back the way they had come through the long gallery. She led them down another wing of the manor with more paintings to a parlor overlooking the front of the house. She opened the double doors to a white and gold room full of cabinets with glass shelves with row after row of porcelain treasures.

"I have ancient Chinese and Japanese porcelain ware in the cases on the right and my German, French, Swiss and other European ware is on the left. Our English ware is in the center, here: Cheslea, Derby, Littledean, Staffordshire, Wedgewood, Worcester and so on."

"Hard paste or soft paste?" asked the French chicken. He sniffed sharply. He bobbed up and down like a chicken pecking for food as he leaned forward to examine one piece, then another, his hands clasped behind his back.

"Both and bone china, and examples of all the various experiments," she said with a laugh. "Most of these pieces are on loan from the Littledean Fine Porcelain collection."

"Might we see the sketches, now?" asked a bored Lady Peverley.

"I, too, vould like to zee zis sketch room," said Herr Doktor Burkholdt. "Zat is vhy you invite me here and zat is vhy I come, to zee de Michelangelos."

"Of course. We can go there now," said the Duchess, though her tone had lost some of its serenity. Ann knew she loved the porcelains and wanted others to appreciate them, too.

She led them further down the hall to double doors on the left. The footman hurried before her to open the doors. She smiled and dipped her head toward him, then turned to lead the party into the room. She turned toward her guests.

And screamed.

CHAPTER 10

THE GREEN PARLOR

The footman who'd opened the doors pushed past everyone to get to the Duchess. She pointed to the corner.

Jacob Holbein lay face down, the back of his head soaked in blood.

Miles and Ann ran to the man. Miles felt for his pulse. "He's not dead. Someone send for a doctor," Miles said.

Everyone stood still, staring in horrified fascination at the bloodied young Holbein laying on the carpet.

"Go!" Miles roared in frustration, surprising himself.

The footman, satisfied the Duchess was all right, turned to the group and spoke to them with an unexpected air of command. "Lady Oakley, if you would be so kind as to fetch Mrs. Weaver and have her bring a bowl of water and rags. Mr. Nowlton, please have one of the stableboys fetch the doctor. The rest of you return to the gold parlor. I will have staff attend to you there and get you all what you might need to overcome this madness. I will assist Lord Redinger."

Everyone responded to his air of command without thought.

Miles pulled off his cravat to press it against Jacob's wound, but Ann pushed his hand back.

"There are shards of porcelain that need to be picked out before we can apply pressure to the wound."

"Porcelain!" Miles looked around. The top half of a porcelain statue lay on the floor three feet away, the bottom half shattered, pieces lying all around Holbein. "It's the missing statue from the gold parlor."

"What?" Ann asked. She looked then at the pieces she'd gathered in her hand from Holbein's head. Tears sprung to her eyes at the destruction of her aunt's beautiful piece. "Yes, it is. What is it doing in here?"

The footman led the Duchess to a chair facing away from the injured man, then he came over to them. "I heard you say this is the statue you discovered missing."

"Yes."

The footman ran a hand through his hair. "Bloody hell. Danger to the Duchess I expected, not to another guest."

"Who are you?" Miles sharply asked.

"Lewis Martin from Bow Street."

"Bow Street!" Ann almost shrieked.

"Yes. Mr. Nowlton contacted me two weeks ago out of concern for his mother. The Duchess has been getting threatening messages for the past month. She does not take them seriously. She refused to cancel this house party, so I am here, much to her irritation, as bodyguard and investigator."

"Do you think the attack on Mr. Holbein is related to these threatening messages?"

"How can I think otherwise, as she has not invited the cream of art society to this event? She has invited just the sorts who would try threats. She's determined to flush out the person behind the threats. And you know, there is no naysaying a duchess."

Mrs. Weaver bustled into the room with the bowl of water and a towel over her arm.

"Poor man, poor man!" she exclaimed. She sank to the floor next to Ann. "I'll take over now, miss. 'Tis is not the sight nor the activity for a young lady such as yourself." She dipped the cloth in the bowl, then wrung it out.

"I think I got all the porcelain shards out of his wound, but you should have a care to look for more," Ann said, moving back. "I might have missed some slivers in the blood."

"Yes, miss. Not to worry. I've cared for more than one bashed head in my time."

Miles stood up and helped Ann to her feet. She went over to her grandmother. She grabbed her hand, then kneeled on the floor beside her chair.

"I really thought it all a hum," her grandmother said softly. "A to-do over a minor work by Michelangelo. Sketches—no—more like simple studies for another painting. Illustrative of how the artist approached his larger paintings, but worth threats?"

"Are they the sketches we brought back from Sicily?"

"Yes, and that was two years ago! If someone wanted them, why wait so long to try to acquire them? And I probably would have sold them at that time. I received so much from Lady Travis I had to sell off some of it. It could have just as easily been the sketches as the other prints and paintings Nowlton sold for me in his gallery."

"I don't understand how Aunt Elizabeth's statue came to be in this print room," Ann said.

"Is that what he was hit with?" her grandmother asked. She sighed. "That was me who moved the statue," she tiredly confessed.

"You!"

"Yes, Georgie—Lady Oakley—and I thought it a lark to move things around and see who noticed. It has been vexing the staff, which has been interesting. Can you believe some have whispered of ghosts? We have had such a laugh. We had more mischief planned with moving things around, but I guess this will put a halt to that. Pity."

"You do realize Elizabeth's statue has been destroyed."

"Yes. I mourn that loss. That was one of her first hard paste porcelain pieces. It brought her and Josiah together!"

"Here, Mother, I have brought you a restorative," Nowlton said, returning to the room. He handed her a small glass of fortified wine and turned to where Miles, the footman, and the housekeeper were tending to the young man who had begun to groan and return to consciousness. "I've sent Jem Pritchard to fetch the doctor. He harnessed the gig, so there should be no delay in fetching the doctor here. Lady Oakley is seeing to the other guests."

"Thank heaven for Georgie. She is a dear. I wouldn't trust some of them not to rob me blind. She will keep them in line, and they won't even realize she has done so."

"Like the Raven and the French Chicken?" Ann asked.

"The what?"

She laughed self-consciously at her automatic use

of the names Miles gave them. "That is what His Grace calls those two collectors who sometimes seem at odds with each other, then as tight as two peas in a pod."

"Lord Wolfred and Sir Robert?" her grandmother asked. She laughed. "I can see Wolfred as the Raven, but Renouf as a Chicken?

"Beg pardon, Your Grace, that was ill done of me. I couldn't place him and all I could think of was a black French Crèvecœur chicken, dressed all in black as he does, and with that wild black hair which reminded me of the crest on the Crèvecœur."

The Duchess laughed. "Now I shall forever see the Crèvecœur black chicken when I meet Sir Robert!"

"My head— Vat happened?" Jacob asked. The quasi-footman helped him to sit up. Mrs. Weaver had placed a pad against his head, held in place by Miles' cravat.

"Why were you in this room?" Lewis asked. "Her Grace had not introduced the guests to this room. Were you meeting someone?"

"Meet zome one? Nein, nein. I try to zee da sketches bevore anyone else."

"So you could steal them?"

"Nein, nein!" He tried to pull away from Mr. Martin and stand up. "I am no zeif," he wailed.

"Oh, let the boy up," the Duchess said. She rose unsteadily to her feet, Ann rose to stand beside her. "We need him carried to a room. Mrs. Weaver, is there a room available in the old family wing on this floor?"

"Yes, Your Grace, I had it prepared in case there were unexpected guests."

Her Grace smiled. "Ah, you are remembering that time after Bertram's death when we had more visitors than expected for the funeral."

"I was."

"Excellent." She looked up at men. "Nowlton, you and the others take him to your grandmother's old room and wait for the doctor. Mrs. Weaver, please have one of the maids clear away the broken statuary and clean up the blood and get as much as possible out of the rug." She sighed as she looked down at the blood-stained rug, then up to where the Michelangelo sketches hung, mute witnesses to the violence in the room. "And make sure the door is locked when they are finished."

~

"WHAT DO you mean by keeping us in here?" demanded Lord Druffner when Ann and the Duchess joined the others in the gold parlor.

"Keeping you here? I haven't kept you anywhere. I dare swear it is your curiosity that has kept you all rooted here," the Duchess said.

"There might be a *murderer* among us," Lady Druffner dramatically declared.

"Murderer? Piffle. The young man is not dead, and he has regained consciousness. He is bleeding, in pain, and confused. The doctor is on the way."

"So, we can see the sketch room now?" Lord Wolfred asked.

The Duchess scowled at him. "No, Lord Wolfred. It is not fit for guests," she said impatiently. "There is blood and broken shards of porcelain on the floor below the Michelangelo sketches. The maids will clean the room today."

"Why would someone hit him?" Sir Robert asked.

"We don't know and at the moment, the young

man cannot tell us much. All he said is, like you, he wanted to see the sketches."

"This would not have happened," grumbled Sir Robert, the French Chicken, "if you had taken us to that room first."

The Duchess slid a sideways glare at him.

"What I'd like to know," Ann said, "is who did not visit the porcelain room?"

"We were all there," Lady Peverley said peevishly.

"Did anyone notice that Mr. Holbein was not with us?" Ann asked.

The guests looked at each other.

"I believe we can all agree Sir Robert was there as he alone went down the rows and peered into the cases at the porcelain displays."

"Thank you," that gentleman said austerely, his corset creaking as he bowed. "I have a profound appreciation for beauty in all art forms. . . unlike some," he said pointedly, staring at his nemesis, Lord Wolfred.

Lord Wolfred sneered and turned his back to him, taking a seat in a winged chair near the fireplace.

"So, what is the plan now?" asked Lord Peverley.

"I cannot offer you entertainments this afternoon as I know I shall be in discussions with the doctor and the young man who broke the rules. As such, you are free to wander the galleries we visited today, including the old abbey. Remember, I am looking to turn the manor into a museum so any suggestions as to my art curation are appreciated. It is too bad I have to close the green parlor for today. I believe it is the room in the most need of renovation in order to properly display sketches and etchings. I know the color of the room threatens to overpower everything within it, I just can't think as to how it should be arranged. I am looking forward to your input," the Duchess said.

Ann thought it unlikely that her grandmother would listen to any ideas but her own; however, she had curiously been on this refrain all day. She was laying on the helplessness a bit strong. Ann considered it quite strange and wondered if perhaps her grandmother was showing signs of senility. She couldn't believe that was the case. Her grandmother had always been too clever.

"Pardon me, Your Grace," said the under footman from the doorway. "A luncheon is ready in the dining room."

"Thank you, John. She turned toward her guests. "I think a bite to eat should do us all well." She led the way to the dining room. At the doorway, she stopped and held Ann back. "Please find out how things are going with Mr. Holbein and let me know. I shall have to stay here and be the smiling hostess. Bother. I thought this would be easy!"

"What would be easy?" Ann asked.

"What? Oh, nothing. Just this house party and everything."

"Grandmother, we need to talk," Ann said severely.

"Oh, listen to you, now. No matter, I'm proud of you," her grandmother said, patting her arm. "Now find out about Mr. Holstein."

"Holbein."

"Oh yes, yes. Holbein. Bring me word how he does."

Ann had a suspicion that her grandmother was trying to get rid of her. Was she saying things to the other guests she did not want her to hear? Nonsense.

She walked down the hall to the old family quarters. She knew why her grandmother thought to sequester Mr. Holbein here. The room that was once great-grandmother's locked on the outside. Before her death, great-grandmother would wander outside at all times of day or night and in all weather with little clothing. Whenever she slept, on waking she would begin to ramble. One night when there was a houseful of guests, she'd gotten turned around, walked up the stairs, and tried to get in bed with one of the young male guests—Ann's father, Graham Hallowell, before he courted her mother. Her horrified grandfather had a lock installed on her bedroom door the next day.

Not knowing if Mr. Holbein was truly a victim or a brigand, her grandmother thought to have him locked in the room.

~

THE DOOR to the bedroom stood ajar when Ann approached. She heard the rumble of Dr. Martin Birdsall's voice as he talked to Mr. Holbein.

She knocked lightly on the door and peeked around the opening.

"Grandmother sent me," she said when several pairs of eyes looked in her direction. Besides Mr. Holbein and the doctor, Miles, Nowlton, Mr. Martin and John the under footman were in the room. It wasn't a big room. With so many men, it was crowded.

Dr. Birdsall nodded. "Quite right. Inform Her Grace that the young man will require a few stitches. He should remain abed for at least three days—"

"Three days!" protested Mr. Holbein. He started to lift his head, grimaced, and flopped back down against the pillows in mute testament to the pain and the reason for remaining in bed.

"Yes, three days," returned Dr. Birdsall, looking back at his patient, "to ensure any concussion subsides," he turned back toward Ann, "and if afterward he feels the least bit dizzy, he should return to his bed. But he appears a hearty enough fellow, so I don't anticipate that."

The doctor clasped his hands together. "Now, I shall require a basin of warm water, a towel, and some brandy."

"I'll fetch them, sir," John said. He hurried from the room.

Nowlton laughed shortly. "John doesn't handle blood well."

"Anything else, doctor?" Ann asked from where she stood by the open door.

"I require two gentlemen to remain and hold him down while I stitch him up."

"Lewis and I will stay," said Nowlton. "Redinger, you can go back to the Duchess with Ann to report on our patient."

Ann felt her heart race at her uncle's words; however, she tamped the reaction down. "Will the patient require any food restrictions?"

"Only for today, broth and weak tea. Tomorrow he can have anything he thinks he can keep down."

"I'll inform cook. Any laudanum?" she pressed.

The doctor shook his head. "I'd rather he not today; however, if it turns out he can't sleep because of too much pain, he can have a little. Sleep is healing, so he'll need his sleep."

"Excellent," she said.

She and Miles left the room together. "Did he say anything?" Ann asked Miles as they walked down the hall.

"You mean about his presence in the Green Parlor?

No. But it was certainly a surprise to find our cheeky head footman is actually a Bow Street agent."

"Yes! I need to question Aidan about what is going on. I can't help but be a bit piqued. It seems this entire house party, including my so-called potential engagement, was merely a ruse for something else. I don't like being used in that manner. That is what went on when we went to Sicily. That was a ruse as well. We provided cover for my uncle and his dealings."

"You mentioned that earlier, then Colonel Brantley cut you off."

"My uncle was a spymaster. While that is a well-known secret now, it wasn't during the wars with Napoleon. He had spies based in Italy. He decided he need to get closer to his spies in Italy as there was a rumor of a traitor in their midst."

"Was there?"

"What?"

"A traitor in his spy network."

She sighed. "Yes. And that is why Lord Harry Blessingame was killed. I don't know if they caught the traitor. My uncle wasn't forthcoming. I know he wasn't happy with events in Sicily and sped up our departure by a week."

"But to track a traitor, he took you, your cousin, the Duchess, and his wife on a family trip to Sicily, in the midst of the war with Napoleon, as a screen for his activities."

"That has always been Uncle Candelstone's way. He will take people to the brink of disaster to achieve his goals."

John was coming toward them down the hall, looking down at the basin of water he held. They stepped to the side out of the earnest young man's way.

When he saw them, he jolted, spilling some water over the edge of the basin.

"Beg pardon, miss, I didn't see you. There is a letter for you on the silver salver by the door. The groom brought it from the village when he fetched Dr. Birdsall."

"Thank you, John," Ann said. She crossed toward the table to get her letter. "I have no notion of who might be writing me here!"

"Except for my cousin."

She made a face. "Yes. And it looks to be from him."

She held it out for Miles to see. "Yes, that is his hand, and franked with the Earl's signet."

"Another poem?" she suggested.

"Most likely. Best you let me read it first."

"Oh, I don't think that will be necessary, not after the dressing down you said you gave him. He will be circumspect, I imagine." She lifted the wax seal and unfolded the letter.

"Yes, it is a poem," she said, laughing. She passed it to Miles after reading it. "Certainly beyond reproach — if not a little plagiarized in a phrase or two."

To my Nymph
She walks in beauty into the light
This nymph, this sprite of delight.
With maidenly charms and meek demeanor
Where she goes flowers bloom and grass is greener.
I long to be where she stays
So we might mark the days
Until hearts and minds are one
And we may be joined as one.

"He does get ahead of himself with his assumptions. You seriously are not still considering marrying him, are you?"

Ann shrugged. "I have to do something."

Miles grabbed her by her shoulders and turned her around to face him. "Miss Hallowell," he began.

A pounding on the door interrupted him.

John ran past them to answer the door.

A large gentleman in the attire of a London professional stood at the door. He handed his card to John. "Mr. and Mrs. Quesinberry and our daughter, Miss Julia Quesinberry. We are expected."

John looked at the card then at the visitors. "Y-yes. Of course," he stammered.

Ann came around John. "Hello, welcome to Versely Park," she said smoothly. She had no idea who these people were; however, they said they were expected. Ann believed them.

"Come in, please come in. 'Tis a trifle breezy outside today," she remarked as they entered.

"Yes, it is," said Mrs. Quesinberry as she entered. She smiled tentatively at Ann.

Ann smiled welcomingly back.

"That is quite the loveliest pelisse I've seen this season," Ann said to the young woman who followed behind her parents. She couldn't have been more than seventeen or eighteen. She was quite lovely. Not beautiful in the current mode, but lovely with vibrant, wavy red hair that curled riotously around the edges of her bonnet. She had a charming heart-shaped face sprinkled with freckles and beautifully clear light brown eyes framed by dark lashes.

"Thank you," the young girl said, scarcely above a whisper. She smiled as tentatively as her mother had and looked down. Ann found the family quite endearing. She wondered where they fit with her grandmother's house party plans.

Mr. Quesinberry!" her grandmother said, coming from the dining room. "Welcome!" she looked over at John. "Please inform Mrs. Weaver more of our guests have arrived." She turned back to the newcomers. "We will get you to your rooms quickly. Are you hungry? Can I get any refreshments for you?"

"No, thank you, your Grace," said Mr. Quesinberry. "We took the journey in easy stages as my daughter is easily carriage sick. We had a large breakfast at the inn where we stayed last night."

"It would be nice to freshen up," Mrs. Quesinberry ventured. "That wind does make one feel grimy after a while."

"That it does! It is often breezy here, so I do know what you mean. But let me introduce you to our other guest here while we are waiting for Mrs. Weaver," she said, noting Miles standing off to the side observing the new guests.

"This is my granddaughter, Miss Ann Hallowell, and the young man standing to the side is the son of an old friend, Viscount Redinger."

"No!" wailed Miss Quesinberry.

There was a beat of surprised silence.

"No! That's not Sebastian!" she screamed. "What have you done with my Sebastian?" She flew at Miles and flailed at him with her gloved fists.

He grabbed her hands to stop her feeble assault, which only infuriated the beauty more.

"Julia! Julia!" her father cried out, pulling her away from Miles.

She collapsed against her father, crying. Her mother came up to her and handed her a handkerchief.

Julia! Here was Redinger's Juliet! Miles was sure of it. He tossed back his head and laughed. "You are quite right, Miss Quesinberry, I am not my cousin, Sebastian Redinger," he said, struggling to regain his composure.

"Cousin?" demanded Mr. Quesinberry? "What manner of jest is this?" he demanded.

"It's a very poor jest," said his wife.

"Oh, I am so sorry," the Duchess said. "This is all my fault. Just a little joke. This is the Duke of Ellinbourne, Viscount Redinger's cousin."

Miss Quesinberry buried her face deeper into her mother's shoulder.

"He came in Redinger's stead as his cousin met with an accident in London."

Miss Quesinberry raised her head. "My Sebastian hurt?" she asked. She hiccupped. "Oh, no!" She wailed, buried her face again, and cried harder.

Mr. Quesinberry looked helplessly at her.

"I assure you, Miss Quesinberry, he bears more bruises than anything else," Miles hastily said. "He shall be right as rain in a few days."

The Duchess sighed. "I supposed I shall have to come clean to everyone now. I so enjoyed having you as not you," she told Miles. "Not that you as you is bad, mind you. It's just that you as you might be awkward here with these collectors. I feared they would not give you peace; however, you as Redinger they would ignore."

Miles shook his head at this confusing speech.

Mrs. Weaver hurried forward.

"Could you show these lovely people to their rooms? Thank you— and the Duke is the Duke again."

She turned to the Quesinberrys. "Please allow

Mrs. Weaver to get you settled. We'll have you bags sent up as soon as they arrive. I take it they and your servants are in a separate carriage? Good," she said on Mr. Quesinberry's nod. "We will expect to see you for tea, then."

The Duchess watched them go up the stairs, then turned to Ann and Miles.

"Grandmother," Ann said in a hushed tone. "Who are the Quesinberrys? They are not collectors as well, are they?"

"Oh, no, no. Mr. Quesinberry is a younger brother of the Earl of Berry. When it came time for him to make his way into the world, he went into law. He is my solicitor."

"Solicitor!"

"Yes, I asked them here for, well, you know," her grandmother said half apologetically.

"For settlements," Ann said flatly.

"Yes." Her grandmother confounded Ann by looking embarrassed. Nevertheless, this was appalling.

"I had not even met Viscount Redinger, and you were thinking of settlements?" Ann asked, outraged. "Without knowing if we would suit? I can tell you right now, we would not have suited."

"So Nowlton told me before the house party, and I see that now."

"And just what is you see?" Ann demanded. Though she knew she was acting disrespectful to her grandmother, she couldn't help the storm of angry emotions.

She knew those emotions had been building, ebbing, then building again and again, ever since Ursula first told her of the plan with Redinger. She had not liked having her life arranged for her in quite that manner; however, she felt conflicted as she wanted her stepmother to marry again and not feel duty bound to her stepdaughter. A marriage of convenience had seemed reasonable, but not to a man who was in love with another!

She closed her eyes a moment.

"I have stated I will consider an arranged marriage. It will not be where there is not at least friendship," she said quietly.

"Well, yes, and you have that here," she said, indicating Miles with the wave of her hand.

"But he's not Redinger."

"No. Better I think."

"Grandmother!" Ann shrieked, color flooding her face. She covered her face with her hands. "Argh!"

Miles stepped forward. "That's what I was going to tell you—to ask you—before the Quesinberrys arrived.

"See!" the Duchess said triumphantly. "Everything for the best."

"No!" Ann said. "I can't just switch from one person to another like that. The viscount has expectations! He even sent me a love poem today."

"He did?" exclaimed the Duchess.

"Yes," Ann said, picking up the letter from where she dropped it on the hall table when she went to greet the Quesinberrys. "See!"

Her grandmother took the missive from her and read it. She grimaced. "Well, I suppose one must give the boy points for effort. But if he loves his Miss Quesinberry—"

"I believe he does," interrupted Miles. "He told me he lost his Juliet, so he didn't care who he married. Miss Hallowell was as good as any."

Ann winced.

"Better because his mother approved. If this Miss Julia Quesinberry is actually his Juliet, which I can believe with the poetic license he has taken lately, I would like to know why did he lose her?"

"Maybe we can set things to right—at least for Miss Quesinberry and your cousin," the Duchess said.

"I'll send an express to him. Bruised face or not, he needs to get here," said Miles.

"Agreed, and you can turn your attention to your opportunity," the Duchess said.

"Wait! You are both moving much too fast for me," said Ann.

"Nonsense, girl. Keep up!" said the Duchess, a gleam in her eye.

CHAPTER 11

A DUCHESS'S MACHINATIONS

W hile her grandmother rejoined her guests and
the duke went off to pen his letter to his
cousin, Ann made her way slowly up the carpeted
stairs. She occasionally paused to look at one or another of the portraits of her relations along the staircase, but she didn't really see them. She felt tumbled
about inside as the revelation that came with the
Quesinberry's presence replayed itself.

Was the Viscount really in love with another?

She owned she could not remember meeting the
viscount, though she'd been told she had as a child.
And she'd honestly not held any expectations they
would suit, though she'd hoped they would as it
would resolve so many issues. With all that, she still
found her spirits quite lowered at the knowledge that
she was somehow a *make-do* wife prospect.

What woman would want to be a *make-do*? She
considered that worse than second best.

And now the Duke was suggesting she marry him
instead in what she was certain was also a *make-do*
wife prospect. He knew she wanted to marry in order
to encourage her stepmother to do the same, and she

was counting on Viscount Redinger to be her husband. It would be convenient for all.

But if the Viscount truly loved Julia Quesinberry, he should marry the woman he loved, not her. He would be miserable and, therefore, so would she. She was already miserable.

And here was the Duke, one of the most courteous men that she had ever met, being quite gentlemanly and saving face for both his cousin and her. No, it would not do. Besides, no doubt the family had expectations of who should be his wife. He could look much higher than a mere Miss Hallowell.

But how had Redinger *lost* Miss Quesinberry? That is what she wanted to know.

Perhaps a kind visit and sympathetic ear would help Miss Quesinberry—and herself.

She found herself staring absently at the portrait of her great-aunt Victoria Nowlton with her frowning countenance. It was like she was frowning directly at her. Family stories said she'd been a spinster and shunted from family member to family member. No wonder she frowned. *Poor woman*, Ann thought. She did not want to end up like her. She sighed. With her trick knee that prevented her from dancing, and the scar on her chin marring her image, she was not a woman that men sought out. Her dowry was modest, but at least she had a dowry. Unfortunately, it was not enough for her to live on if she did not marry.

Still, to marry the Duke? She smiled to herself as she resumed her slow climb up the stairs. He was a delightful man. His humor matched her own. It was a great deal too bad he had to go and inherit the dukedom. She could have been quite happy as an artist's wife.

What was she thinking? She needed to rein in her thoughts.

She went down the hall of the first floor to the west wing. They would have their rooms there. There was a nice suite of rooms suitable for a family in that wing. She heard the rumble of a man's voice, Mr. Quesinberry. It came from the parlor that stood between the two bedrooms. She knocked quietly on the door.

Mr. Quesinberry opened the door, his expression stern. His large frame filled the doorway. He looked down at her. Ann did not consider herself a small woman; however, as he looked at her, his expression as unyielding as the professional solicitor he was, Ann suddenly felt tiny and awkward.

"I—I thought perhaps Miss Quesinberry would like someone to talk to. The Duke pretending to be his cousin must have been a huge shock. I—I thought I could tell her how it came to be. . . ." Her voice awkwardly trailed off.

His stern expression relaxed. "It is a devil of a muddle, isn't it?" he kindly said. "We were discussing this. I was just learning how much my dear wife and daughter have kept from me!—And, perhaps me from them, too." He shook his head dolefully. "Please, do come in, Miss Hallowell." He opened the door wider and stood aside.

"Thank you," she said.

In the parlor Mrs. Quesinberry and Miss Quesinberry sat on the sofa. Mrs. Quesinberry held her daughter against her, rocking gently back and forth as she must have done when her daughter was an infant.

"Miss Quesinberry?" Ann said as she walked toward the couple.

Julia Quesinberry glanced at her, then again began wailing.

"Please. Might we talk?" Ann asked. "I suspect something odd has happened."

"He said he didn't want to see me anymore," said her muffled voice from against her mother.

"Who said?" Ann asked.

"That man! Isn't that right, Mama?" Julia said, raising her head to look at her mother.

Mrs. Quesinberry nodded. "Yes." She looked at Ann. "He sent his butler to us! Of all the effrontery! To inform my gentle Julia that he could not see her anymore. That he was mistaken in his affections."

"Was there any note from Viscount Redinger?"

"Yes, just a short one saying goodbye. *That man* said the viscount was too *busy* to write more," declared Mrs. Quesinberry.

"What? No, no! I don't believe that."

"I had no notion that my Julia had met Viscount Redinger," Mr. Quesinberry said. "I knew she had met a gentleman she was attracted to, but nothing beyond that. My wife and daughter were not forthcoming. Though in their defense, I will say I was too busy with my work to pay proper attention to my daughter. As a solicitor, I know details matter, yet I didn't ask."

"The Duke, his cousin, said the Viscount has been in the mopes because he could not find you, and that is why he agreed to a marriage of convenience with me," Ann told Julia.

Her young face crumpled.

"He called you his Juliet," Ann said gently. "We must discuss this with the Duke. I do not wish to be a convenience, and under the circumstances I can't conceive for whom the convenience might be!"

Mr. Quesinberry laughed but cut it off when his wife glared at him. He cleared his throat. "I did wonder why the Duchess wanted me to draw up settlement documents between you and Viscount Redinger. I wasn't aware of my daughter's attachment to the gentleman."

"I believe the marriage suggestion was started with correspondence between the Duchess, my stepmother, and Lady Galborough."

"That wretched man did allude to Lady Galborough's displeasure," Mrs. Quesinberry said.

Mr. Quesinberry frowned. "There shouldn't be any problem with my Julia's antecedents, as she is the granddaughter of an earl. And she has a ten thousand pound dowry from my mother, the Countess of Berry, as she is her only granddaughter. My mother has quite spoiled Julia over the years," he confided to Ann with another laugh.

"As I said, something is not right. We will get this sorted out. The Duke is sending a letter to his cousin. He would have been here; however, it is my understanding he was injured in a mishap late one evening while out drowning his sorrows." Ann didn't know if he was drowning any sorrows or not. Soothing this distraught young woman was more important.

"My stepmother asked the Duke to join us in his stead to balance the numbers. The Duke told me his cousin enthusiastically endorsed the plan. That does not sound like a man intent on signing settlements immediately if he could countenance someone else coming for him. That is more in the way of a delaying strategy."

"But why was the Duke saying he was my Sebastian?" Julia asked, her voice like that of a small child.

"That was my grandmother's prank." She looked up at Mr. Quesinberry. "If you have done work for the Duchess for any length of time, you would know how she loves to set the cat amongst the pigeons."

Mr. Quesinberry nodded. "I do indeed. I had wondered if this invitation here weren't another of her machinations."

"Claiming the Duke was the Viscount was a spur-of-the-moment action. The opportunity presented itself and she couldn't resist."

"That does sound like the Duchess," Mr. Quesinberry prosaically agreed.

"I think it sounds quite horrid, Mr. Quesinberry," declared his wife.

"If this didn't involve our dear Julia, you would see the humor in this," he assured her. "Julia, dry your tears. We must make an appearance downstairs with the other guests. Until we know more, as Miss Hallowell suggests, you must display a calm I know you will not feel."

"As this story gets around, as you know it will, you will be quite revered for your fortitude in this trying situation," Ann suggested, though privately she knew the guests below were not the sympathetic sort, with an interest only in art. Nonetheless, as her purpose was to make this poor girl feel better, a little stretching of the truth stood to a good cause. Julia was quite young and naive. Ann felt ages her elder.

"I look to see you all downstairs later. Thank you for seeing me now," Ann said.

She turned to leave them. Mr. Quesinberry was before her to open the door.

"My thanks to you, dear lady," he said quietly.

She smiled at him and shrugged slightly before she passed out of the room.

~

ANN FOUND Miles in the library writing a letter.

"Haven't you sent off the letter to your cousin yet?"

"Yes, I got that off right away. The Duchess had a groomsman take it personally to London to see that it gets into Sebastian's hands as soon as possible."

"Do you think he will come here?"

"Yes, I do, especially as I told him I thought his Juliet was an excellent match. This letter I am composing is to my aunt and uncle. I am considering how to approach this matter."

"I discovered how it was that Miss Quesinberry disappeared."

Miles set the quill down and leaned back in his chair. "Indeed?"

"Yes," Ann said. She sat down across from him. "It was because of Viscount Redinger's butler!"

"Randolph?"

"I don't know his name, just that a gentleman claiming to be Redinger's butler paid a call on them and informed Mrs. Quesinberry and Miss Quesinberry that the Viscount wanted to cancel their next plans to meet. He decided he was mistaken in his affections."

"Was there a note from Sebastian?"

"Yes, but very brief. The butler said the viscount did not have time to sit down to right a longer note."

Miles frowned angrily. "That would not be Sebastian under any circumstances. I will see that Randolph is sacked! What in bloody hell—excuse me, Miss Hallowell—what could make the man do that?"

"I don't know.—Unless he was asked to?"

"Hmph." His eyes narrowed. "I can see Lord Galborough setting a watchdog on his son. Galborough is a strict and stern man, certain of only one way to do things, and that is his way. He tried to order me to get rid of my paints and canvas when I inherited the

Ellinbourne title. His wife gently reminded him that I was of higher rank now and ordering me to do his bidding was not done. At that he looked as if he'd eaten a particularly sour fruit."

Ann laughed. "When was this?"

"At the reading of the will after my uncle's death." He sat straighter in his chair and looked down at the letter. "Now how might I use the information about Randolph to the best advantage?"

"Here's another thing I discovered. Her grandmother, the Countess of Berry well dowered her, as she had only sons and Miss Quesinberry is her only granddaughter."

"That will certainly get their attention!"

"I will leave you to it then. I mean to go have a word or two with Grandmother to ensure we have her support."

"Excellent notion. I have a feeling we already do."

Ann grinned. "I know."

IN THE GOLD PARLOR, Ann was surprised to find the Marquis of Peverley lecturing the other guests, including Herr Doktor, on print collecting and folio albums in the 18th century. She stood just in the doorway and listened, not wanting to interrupt. The Marquis seemed quite knowledgeable. The guests listened intently, nodding their understanding as he spoke.

"Many collectors in prior centuries glued their prints into albums at the margins," he was saying from where he stood in front of the fireplace. "The Duchess of Northumberland trimmed her prints down to the print itself and made paper tabs, which she glued to the print and then into her albums. I don't like glue to touch my prints. I recommend making paper corners, gluing those into albums, then the print can be held in place in folios by these paper corners," he said.

"Fascinating," the Duchess said. "I wonder why the Michelangelo sketches were not preserved in folios? They were framed when I purchased them from Lady Travis, as were all the prints and sketches she had in her collection. Not that she had a large collection of prints and sketches. She preferred oil paintings."

"Caring for one's collection should not be forgotten," said the Marchioness.

"Agreed.—Ah, there you are, Ann! Are the Quesinberrys getting settled?"

"Yes, and they will join us for tea."

"Excellent. Would you tell Mrs. Weaver we are ready at any time?"

"Of course." Ann slipped back out of the room and almost ran into the footman-Bow Street agent.

"Excuse me, Mr. Martin!"

"No, my fault entirely," he said quietly. "But do call me Lewis as I am still your head footman. It would be best if we keep my purpose here quiet."

"I understand," she said. "Though I'll own, I don't understand your role here."

"Until this morning, I wondered the same." He frowned. "Do you think any of the guests know of the various hidden corridors and priests's holes in this house?"

"Only the ones we showed them this morning. Not many in the family know them all."

His forehead creased as he considered her words. "I'd like to talk to you and Nowlton later."

"Of course. I'm on my way to see Mrs. Weaver about the afternoon tea. Perhaps after tea?"

He nodded.

Ann hurried on and gave Mrs. Weaver her grand-mother's instructions, then went back to the library, but the Duke was no longer there.

She frowned. She had wanted to discuss the attack on Mr. Holbein with him.

She wandered into the library, looking at all the bookcases. Mr. Martin had her thinking of all the hidden places and passages in Versely Park. There were a couple connecting to the library, she thought with a smile as her eyes flitted toward them. She was likely the only person to know all the hidden aspects of the manor house for the reasons she shared with the Duke. And she knew there was one narrow, hidden corridor that led from a small antechamber off the grand entry hall to the green room. But who else might know of that?

She sat down in the old leather wing chair facing the cold fireplace and drew up her feet on the seat.

Mentally she went through her relations. Uncle Arthur, the current Duke of Malmsby, rarely left his library save for meals, sleeping, church, occasional votes in Parliament, and historical lectures. The twins, Guinevere and Lancelot preferred London and Merlin was attending medical school in Edinburgh, Aunt Elizabeth and her husband Josiah Littledean seldom visited Versely Park and Ann admitted she hadn't seen her cousin Helena since the Sicily trip with Grand-mother, Aunt Caroline and her husband, Lord William Candelstone.

Since Lord Candelstone had been a neighbor while growing up, and had for years been a spymaster, she supposed he might know the secret spaces and passages in the house through her Aunt Catherine. Nowlton said she loved to play in them, darting out to surprise her brothers and sisters. Remembering her time in Sicily, Ann found it hard to correlate her sweet, quiet aunt with the hellion her uncle told her about. Still, it was possible she knew more than Nowlton was aware.

She supposed one must consider the servants. There always seemed to be a new face about, and likely some she had never met that came and went. Though most staff stayed for years as the Duchess was easy to work for—except for the occasional prank.

She leaned her head against the chair wing. It was nice to be alone for a few moments. She wasn't used to large groups of people as she and Ursula lived fairly quietly in London. Colonel Brantley was their only regular caller. She thought about her stepmother and the Colonel. They made a good match, despite the age difference. She made him youthful, and he kept her enthusiasms in check.

There were footsteps in the hallway. She hadn't closed the library door, but she hoped whoever was there would pass on. She enjoyed her solitude.

"Have you learned anything?" she heard one man say. It was Colonel Brantley! She was sure of it.

"No. You?" another man asked. She thought that was the Marquis of Peverley; however, she couldn't be sure. He spoke in a sibilant whisper.

"Bloody Hell!" swore Colonel Brantley.

"Sh-sh," hissed the other man. "Tell me, what do you think of this head footman fellow?"

"Overly zealous. Currying the Duchess's favor, I'd say," Colonel Brantley offered.

"Hmm. Maybe. Something is off. Strikes me as too smart for a footman."

Colonel Brantley laughed. "Even servants want to get ahead. Nothing wrong with that. You're jumping at shadows. Let's get back to the parlor before we're missed."

Ann heard them walk off. She waited until she no longer heard footsteps, then she stood up. What was that all about? Did this have anything to do with the threats to her grandmother? Were they also trying to solve that mystery, or were they part of it?

Ann felt a heavy chill in her chest.

CHAPTER 12
A DUKE REVEALED

"Hadley! Come in and meet everyone!" The Duchess called out as the Quesinberrys came in the gold parlor for tea.

She looked at the other guests. "Everyone, this is the Honorable Hadley Quesinberry, his wife Pamela and daughter Julia. We are all informal here, so I will let you make your acquaintance over tea. Too exhausting to do individual introductions right now, especially as I have a confession to make," she said, with a mock contrite expression.

"I have been a mischievous Duchess," she admitted, "and have played a prank on one of our guests here. But he got his revenge by playing along with my game, so I am forced to confess."

The guests looked from one to another, trying to figure out what she was talking about. Ann smiled. She could tell by her grandmother's introduction to her confession that she would get through this prank as she did others.

She walked over to Miles. "This man is not Viscount Redinger," she said, gesturing at him.

"I knew it!" proclaimed Lord Druffner, preening.

"Something too common about the man," he said, nodding and looking to the others for confirmation.

No one made any sign they agreed but were staring intently at the Duchess and Miles.

"The Viscount recently met with an accident in London," the Duchess continued, ignoring Lord Druffner. "There were some injuries: bruising, and a broken arm, I understand."

Miles nodded.

"Mrs. Hallowell suggested, and the Viscount agreed, that his cousin should come in his stead."

"Against the law to impersonate a peer," Lord Druffner growled.

The Duchess glanced at him, then back at Miles. "When I learned of the swap of guests, I pretended he is Viscount Redinger and addressed him as Viscount Redinger and ignored any protestations that he is not the Viscount. And I introduced him to all of you as Viscount Redinger."

"I quite thought the Duchess senile," Miles said, looking up at her, a smile pulling at the corner of his lips.

The Duchess put her hands on her hips. "Now that has me hoisted on my own petard," she admitted to him. She looked up at the guests. "To continue the game of denying him his own identity was naughty of me, so now I must reintroduce him to you by his rightful name and title."

"Title?" repeated Lord Druffner.

"Yes, his title," said the Duchess. She did a theatrical curtsey. "This gentleman is Miles Wingate, the Duke of Ellinbourne."

"Ha ha! That quite has got you, eh, Druffner!" Lord Wolfred exclaimed as he slapped his hand on his knee.

Lord Druffner sneered. "Still wasn't raised to the manner. Cousin, if I remember rightly, and I dare say I do. Got a mind for things like that."

Miles nodded. "Yes, I am a cousin of the last Duke."

"So, everyone here—save for the Quesinberrys—have been part of my prank on the Duke," the Duchess said. "It's been sporting of him to go along with my fun."

The Duchess looked at Ann. "Now see, Ann, I have confessed and it is not the disaster you feared."

"No, Grandmother, indeed it is not, but I think I could use some tea."

The Dowager Duchess blinked. "Of course! That is what we are gathered for! Botsford—"

"IF ANYONE WOULD LIKE MORE, now is the time to get it. I have a surprise for you," the Duchess announced to her guests as they sipped tea and nibbled on the cakes and scones her cook had prepared for the afternoon.

Ann's heart dropped to her stomach. Such statements were often preludes to her grandmother's bits of roguery. They had recovered nicely from the Duchess's revelation of the Duke's true identity. Even Lord Druffner seemed to have recovered from his sulks. What now?

She looked across the room at her uncle. He wore a guarded expression. Ann deduced he had the same foreboding. When she looked toward Miles, he was looking at her, his expression quizzical. She shrugged. Only the Bow Street Runner looked at ease. She looked back at her grandmother, who was attempting a haughty, bored demeanor; however, Ann could tell she was bursting with excitement.

"My staff informs me that the carpet below where my Michelangelo sketches hang may not be dry by tomorrow."

"But—" Lord Druffner began to protest. The Duchess raised her hand.

"I decided to remove the sketches from the green parlor and bring them here for you to see."

"You have them here?"

"I do."

Whispers blew through the room like a strong garden breeze.

"Where!"

"Let's see them!"

"If this is another of your tricks—"

"Hush, hush, all of you. Lewis, if you would be so kind?"

The footman walked over to the cabinet next to the fireplace and pulled a framed piece from below. He held it in two hands as he walked first to Lord Wolfred and Sir Robert Renouf who were the closest to him.

Lord Wolfred grabbed it eagerly from him and Sir Robert leaned in to view it. "Exquisite!" said Lord Wolfred, his eyes moving over the entire sketch.

"Turn it over, turn it over," said Sir Robert excitedly.

Paper covered the back, glued in place. Sir Robert scraped at a corner with his thumb nail. "If I can—"

A hand clamped around his wrist.

"What?—How dare you grab a peer of the realm!" protested Sir Robert when he saw it was the footman with his hand about his wrist.

"He dares because my instructions to him were to

make sure no one harmed the sketches in any way. And you are not a peer of the realm, you are a knight of the realm," said the Duchess. "Lewis," she said, "let go of his wrist and take the sketch from them. They have lost their opportunity for study with their disrespect."

"Your Grace," Sir Robert said, outraged, "a collector always looks over art pieces, including the back before they make a purchase. It is only prudent."

"And I have said on numerous occasions that the sketches are not for sale, have I not?" returned the Duchess.

"Preposterous!" objected Sir Robert. "Everything has a price."

"Perhaps, given the right time and occasion; however, this is neither."

"Why take the sketch away from me?" protested Lord Wolfred.

"You were ready to let him rip the paper away from the back of the frame. You were complicit in his actions." She turned to the footman still holding the sketch. "Lewis, you may allow the Peverleys to view the sketch. The same rules apply," she said, more for the Peverleys than Lewis.

"Herr Doktor Burkholdt, you will be last, as I know you will want the most time to study the sketch. The same rules will apply to you."

The German bowed his head in understanding. "You do know zat prezice autenication can not happen zwitout de removal vrom de vrame."

The Duchess inclined her head. "Yes. But that is not for today.—If ever," she said. "I find I am distressed that the first people to look at the picture tried to take it out of the frame without permission."

"My enthusiasm overruled my thinking," defended Sir Robert.

"I know. I do not pretend to understand; however, I know."

The Marquis passed the frame to Lord and Lady Druffner. "Even without seeing the back for any dealer or owner marks for provenance, I am inclined to believe it is original. Might we see the second sketch?" he asked.

"Aidan, would you please get the second sketch and take it to the Marquis? I expect you to act as Lewis did if provocation arises."

"Do not worry, Your Grace, it will not," assured Peverley. "I have too much respect for you, unlike others," he said, staring at Sir Robert Renouf.

Sir Robert glared back at him.

"I will allow the pictures to stay in this parlor until dinner, at which time my staff will see they are locked away. There will be additional opportunities to see them tomorrow, along with my collection of prints and sketches. I do not have as extensive a collection as the Marquis; however, I do have some interesting pieces dating to the fourteenth and fifteen centuries. Today we went through the west wing gallery. There is another gallery in the east wing you will be able to explore tomorrow. It lacks the attribute of hidden doors and passageways; however, on its own, it is an interesting gallery."

The Duchess paced in front of the fireplace. Ann recognized the pacing as a residual sign of her agitation. Otherwise, the Duchess was the picture of calm authority.

"My hope is tomorrow afternoon, once this absurd preoccupation with the Michelangelo sketches subsides, you will take a greater degree of interest in my art collections and we can have a discussion on how best to curate everything. Aside from the Druffners, you are experts in the arts, and I value your opinions."

The various guests nodded and preened—as was their wont to do—and rose to leave when their time with the sketches passed. The Peverleys joined Herr Doktor and his wife as they looked at the sketches and softly discussed their thoughts. Lewis hovered nearby.

"Excuse me, Your Grace," Miles said as he too stood to leave, "why do you want to create a museum here? Isn't it the family seat? What about Malmsby or his heir?"

The Duchess nodded. "That is a fair question. Neither Arthur nor Lancelot like the property."

"Hate would be a better term," Nowlton drawled, joining them.

"I think that is too strong. They do have other estates they prefer. But this is the chief estate and does the best for the family financially from the villages and tenant farms that surround us. To let the estate go empty would not help the value of the total property, and to lease the property we would have to ensure the lessee maintained it, and without the rents it may be hard for someone other than an India Nabob to do so! It is an expensive property. Making it a museum will go toward keeping it self-supporting and keeping the locals employed."

"But you are quite a ways from London or other major cities. Why would people come here?" Miles asked.

"I suggested the solution," Nowlton said. "Over the last couple of years, along with the rise of the merchant class, there has been a rise in curiosity by people in the arts, in educational topics and in how the aristocracy lives. I witness this in London at my gallery. When mother mentioned the increase in visitors that come to tour the gardens in the summer, I saw the correlation to what was happening in London. Versely Park is even featured in printed tour guides! A museum would be an added draw. It would do much to dispel the first impression the house gives of a plain waif along with helping to support it."

"I see you have thought on this a great deal."

"Yes, and done financials with our estate agent and our London bankers. Arthur is all for it because he doesn't have to do anything."

"Aidan, you know your brother is a brilliant man and needs to continue his work."

"Mother, do you know what his work is?" Nowlton asked.

"Not exactly, but he is deep into his studies."

"He researches the Arthurian legends because his late wife was a devotee of the old romances. She wanted them to be real, so that is what my dear brother has been trying to do for the past twenty years, prove the legends."

"Well, I guess someone should study them, so why not Arthur?" the Duchess asked.

Nowlton threw up his hands. "Insanity!"

"I find my sympathies are with your brother," Miles said mildly as he scraped at a tiny fleck of paint on his hand left over from the morning's outing. "Your brother's passion for Arthurian legends is no different from my passion for painting." He looked up at Nowlton.

"What I fail to understand is exactly what a Duke is supposed to do? We keep hundreds of people employed doing everything for us save our bodily functions. Providing employment is good for the economy. But what are *we* to do? Why shouldn't a Duke do what he should like to do instead of what others say he should do? Or is our function to only participate in blood sports, wench, carouse, and gamble away our patrimony?" Miles asked.

Silence.

Ann and her grandmother exchanged glances.

A frown creased Nowlton's brow as he stared at Miles. He inhaled deeply. "I beg your pardon, Your Grace," he finally said into the silence. "If you'll excuse me—" He turned and left.

"That was interesting," Ann said.

"Yes," agreed her grandmother. "I've never seen Aidan nonplussed before."

"My apologies, Lady Malmsby," Miles said, looking down, his lips compressed. "The role of a Duke has been a difficult subject for me within my own family. I had no right to take out my frustrations on Mr. Nowlton."

"Nonsense. He needed that dressing down. He will be better for it. I don't want an apology, I want to applaud you! I love my son dearly; however, sometimes he believes he knows better than anyone else. We all have some things to learn from time to time."

"Speaking of doing what I enjoy--" Miles turned toward Ann. "Shall we attempt the sketching exercise again, Miss Hallowell? I believe I saw a likely object for our attention in the library."

"I should like that," she said. "I will check on Mr. Holbein first, then join you directly—unless you have anything else you would rather I do?" Ann asked her grandmother, who had been looking between them with raised eyebrows.

"No, no. Since Lady Oakley seems to have temporarily deserted me for the exercise of keeping Lord Druffner out of trouble—an activity I heartily approve

of—I am going to join the Peverleys and Doktor Burkholdt in the examination of the sketch. I shall see you
at dinner."

"I won't be long," Ann said to Miles when they
reached the entrance hall. "I'll get my sketching materials, pay a visit to Mr. Holbein, then meet you in the
library. I would like to tell you what I overhead earlier
today and see if you can make any sense of it, and if I
should tell Mr. Martin or my uncle."

"If you are wondering, then you probably should.
But I will meet you in the library when you are ready."

MILES PULLED a bronze cupid statue out of a bookcase
niche. It was a charming piece, simple, pleasing to the
eye, the kind of sculpture one would expect to find in
porcelain, not bronze. For their sketches, it would do.
It was signed 'Falconet'. He set it on a table, then
arranged a gas lamp and some candles to provide light
from two angles, one brighter than the other, to give it
depth. When he was satisfied, he sat down to await
Ann, his sketchbook and charcoal beneath his hand.

He thought about her. Sometimes it seemed he
thought about her all the time—and by her given
name. He hoped he didn't slip and call her Ann before
she gave him leave to do so. He feared he might as
much as she consumed his thoughts.

He'd never met a woman with whom he felt comfortable, like he felt with her. He had been attracted to
her like any man might be attracted to a woman with
friendly eyes and a warm smile.

But for him, there was something about her that
pulled him to her. When she was in the same room, he
had a difficult time not staring at her.

Maybe it was her obvious intelligence and humor. His sister, Cassandra, had those attributes. She tried to mask them as she said those facets of a woman's personality were deemed off-putting to a potential husband. He couldn't understand that thinking and was delighted Ann felt no need to repress the humor and intelligence. He enjoyed how often they shared amused glances for circumstances about them.

As a duke—a peer of the realm—they had drilled it into him that he must marry. He accepted that he could not have a life like his Uncle Clarence had had of feckless travel from one location to another to paint, taking commissions when he needed funds to travel to the next place on a map. That would never have been a life for him. He was a quiet man who liked quiet things. Not the personality of a duke, but being a duke was the hand he'd been dealt.

What he said to Nowlton was true. Dukes were still men who might have their own hopes and dreams. If a man did his duty to the title and the responsibilities thrust upon him, might he not pursue his own hobbies?

He'd heard through drawing room rumors the story of the Marquis of Tarkington asking his estate carpenter to teach him to work with wood so he might make his young daughter a rocking horse by his own hands. Society had been shocked and considered his actions a waste of time. Miles thought it was a splendid idea. It was something to inform his own plans if he had children.

No, not if. When.

Again, Ann's face came to him, and not just in his mind, he'd been sketching her likeness as he waited. He looked down at the picture. He'd drawn a detailed picture as he'd sat lost in thought—including her scar.

More pretty than beautiful, her warmth shone through. He'd drawn her head canted slightly to the left, dimples carved into her cheeks and her eyes alight. Her hair was not drawn neat and orderly. She looked more like she had when he'd retrieved her bonnet—windblown and natural.

This was the woman he wanted for his Duchess.

When Sebastian avowed his intentions of taking Miss Quesinberry as his wife—as he was confident he would, Miles would breathe easily and give Ann the courtship she deserved.

He carefully moved the sketch into his portfolio, leaned back in his chair, and stared out the window. Nowlton and Lord Wolfred were walking down the path that led toward the ruined abbey. The Raven's posture and arm gestures suggested he was haranguing Nowlton. Most likely to get him to convince his mother to sell the Michelangelo sketches to him.

Nowlton appeared unruffled and unmoved by the man's intensity. Then he saw Mr. Martin, the erstwhile footman, come out and say something to Nowlton. Nowlton turned to Lord Wolfred, sketched a slight bow, and followed Mr. Martin back into the house.

Wolfred stalked off in the other direction, his posture radiating anger.

Miles wondered why Lord Wolfred was so determined to get the Michelangelo sketches. They were certainly nice enough, but hardly worth his determination. If he were to go to Italy at this time, Miles felt he could purchase other works by Michelangelo for less. Many aristocrats throughout the continent had been selling family heirlooms in an effort to shore up the financial damage wrought by the Napoleonic wars.

ANN HURRIED TOWARD THE LIBRARY. She'd spent more time than she would have liked talking to the doctor about Mr. Holbein's care.

Dr. Birdsall, a talented and well-regarded surgeon, had the unfortunate habit of pontification on matters of treatment. Ann thought he considered his ad hoc lectures expected. And as he was such a nice man, it was difficult to get away from him without seeming rude.

He put seven stitches neatly in the young man's head. She knew they were neat, as he'd insisted he show her! Then he wrapped a soft white cloth around Mr. Holbein's head. He said he'd considered applying leeches but didn't as the bleeding appeared to be sub-siding; however, if he appeared to be bleeding heavily again, then they were to notify him and he would bring leeches. He recommended Indian Saffron tea for his headache now, and laudanum to help him sleep if needed. He could have coffee in the morning, as that sometimes helped with head pain.

She'd promised they would follow his directions as she escorted him to the door, where Jem waited to take him back to the village.

Ann opened the library door and started to close it behind her, then stopped. It would not do to be in a room with the door closed with the Duke. No sense forcing a match as much as she could see herself wed to Miles. She left the door open.

Miles.

When had she started thinking of him as Miles and not Ellinbourne? She silently laughed at herself.

"I'm sorry it took me so long, Your Grace. Dr. Bird-sall would have me know all he had done, and all his medical considerations, in great detail."

Miles rose from his chair and turned to face her.

"Your duties are behind you. Now you can relax. Come. Sit down. I've set up a scenario for us."

Ann laid her art materials on the table and sat down in the chair he indicated. She inhaled deeply.

Yes, now I can relax, she decided.

She looked up at him and smiled. "Thank you."

"Thank me? For what?" Miles asked as he sat down.

"For knowing I need to relax."

"And take your mind in another direction. I have created the opportunity to put thoughts of what is going on with your grandmother and her art gallery planning house guests aside."

"I am anxious to hear it."

"I found this bronze in the shelves," Miles said.

"The Falconet cupid," she said.

"I'm not familiar with Falconet; however, the bronze has a sweet simplicity that will do well for our sketching."

"He was a sculptor in the last century. French, and I believe, worked extensively with Sèvres."

"This did strike me like a subject more often found in porcelain," he said, amused.

"I don't know much about him. I confess I only half listened when Grandmother was instructing me on this statue. I don't have the affinity for sculpture that my aunt and cousin do," she admitted.

"Few artists do well in all medium or enjoy working in all mediums. It can be heavily driven by their need for funds," he said drily.

Ann sighed. "I imagine that would be true."

"Let's do a quick sketch of the bronze now. It is a simple piece and shouldn't take long. Then we can discuss interpretation." He picked up his pencil.

Ann looked at him quizzically. "Interpretation?"

Her expression slammed into him. "Yes," he managed to say. "The different feelings we can portray with our sketches," he said, fighting down the urge to pull her into his arms and kiss her.

Ann didn't know how they would do that, but was open to learning.

"And, to throw a challenge to you," he said, determined to get his wild emotions in control, "while you sketch, tell me what had you concerned earlier."

"While I sketch?" she asked.

"Yes. Concentrating on the sketch will help to remove emotion from your concerns." As he hoped it helped him as well.

Ann thought about that for a moment. She didn't know what the duke could be about; however, it was fun to have a challenge. And she did want to think deeply about the conversation she overheard. She started to draw the outline of cupid and his wings.

"I was here, in the library," she said, "sitting in that chair by the fireplace with my feet drawn up. I was enjoying a moment of serenity away from the house party."

"I can understand that," said Miles, nodding as he, too, sketched the bronze statue.

"The library door stood open. I heard footsteps in the hall. They seemed to come from the estate room. It was two gentlemen conversing. Colonel Brantley, I'm certain, and I think the second man was the Marquis of Peverley."

"Peverley and Brantley?" Miles lifted his charcoal from the paper and stared across the table at Ann. "I wouldn't have thought them to have more than a nodding acquaintance."

"I know. They are so different, right?" Ann said.

"I'm certain it was Colonel Brantley, I am not so certain that the second man was Peverley. The man spoke in a sibilant hissing voice that I think he used in an attempt to disguise his identity in case they were overheard."

"Did you hear what they said?" Miles asked, not looking toward her now, his eyes moving from the statue to his drawing and back.

"Yes," Ann said. "The gentleman who could have been Colonel Brantley asked the second man if he'd heard anything."

"Heard anything?"

"Yes. He answered no, and then he asked Colonel Brantley what he thought of Mr. Martin—though of course he didn't call him Mr. Martin. He called him the footman. The colonel thought he was currying favor with Grandmother. The other gentleman thought there was something off about him. Colonel Brantley seemed to scoff at that idea, said they'd best get back to the parlor before they were missed."

"That is what you heard? All of it?" Miles asked.

"Yes. I waited in the library until I could no longer hear their footsteps, then I followed them out toward the parlor. The Quesinberrys were coming down the stairs so that diverted my attention from seeing who else they may have spoken with before all the guests reassembled."

She set her charcoal aside and gave a little self-conscious laugh. "That was interesting to speak so dispassionately when before I have been tied in a sailor's knot."

"How do you feel about your drawing?"

"Detached."

He laughed. "Yes, it is not a sculpture to elicit strong feelings. Let's change the lighting a bit." He got up and repositioned the light sources for the bronze. Now there were more shadows.

He stood behind her, fighting the urge to place his hands on her shoulders. "Think about your confusion. Let it flood your mind as you start to sketch. Imbue your mind with your confusion. Do not second guess what you are doing. Do not think about how different this sketch is beginning to be from the last, just feel it."

Ann looked at the bronze now layered in shadow. "He does not look happy. He looks cynical," she said as her hands sketched his features. "Reminds me how Nowlton looks sometimes," she mused.

Miles returned to his seat and began sketching the shadowed cupid.

"I saw Nowlton out in the garden with Lord Wolfred. It appeared Wolfred was trying to convince Nowlton of something. Nowlton appeared steadfastly non-committal," he said.

"When was this?" Ann asked.

"While you were dealing with Dr. Birdsall, I presume."

"Nowlton is good at hiding what he thinks and feels. I think that will get him into trouble one day," Ann said. "I believe I am done. I would not have believed it; however, this sketch looks nothing like the last." She pushed the paper forward.

Her cupid's smile now looked like a cynical smirk.

"Just as our drawing can have different emotions, so can our memories and what is happening emotionally colors our memories."

"You are telling me something."

"Yes," he said, looking at her steadily. "You dwell on that accident you had five years ago. It colors how you react to life. Don't let it."

She gave an unladylike snort. "Easy for you to say, Your Grace," she answered formally.

Miles leaned toward her. "Miss Hallowell," he said softly.

Ann's heart beat faster as she stared into his eyes.

The mantle clock chimed the hour.

Ann jumped, startled and embarrassed. "Oh! I hadn't realized how late it is. Excuse me, Your Grace. I have more tasks this evening."

She got up and fairly flew out the library door, leaving Miles looking after her, bemused.

CHAPTER 13

A HIDDEN PASSAGE

S omething woke her.

Ann stared up at the bed-curtains surrounding her bed, visible as shades of black. She blinked and listened.

There it was again, a slight creak.

She recognized it. Someone was in the hidden narrow passage behind her bedroom wall. Long ago, she'd disabled the secret door to this bedroom, as this was the room she commonly stayed in when visiting her grandmother. She hadn't trusted her cousins—or her grandmother—to refrain from using that hidden door for some prank.

She pushed her blankets aside, sat up, and swung her legs to the side of the bed. She didn't pull back the bed curtains. She slipped soundlessly between the panels. She shivered. The room was cold.

She grabbed her wrapper from the chair where she'd tossed it when she went to bed and slipped her feet into her slippers. She carefully made her way to a window and as silently as she could, opened a drapery panel to let in moonlight.

The secret passage led to the abbot's room in the

old monastery. It was the other hidden access to the monastery from this floor. Her room was near the long gallery and a windowless guest bedroom, and two small servant rooms were on the other side of the corridor. Her room and the guest bedroom were the only egress into the passage from the house. Whoever was in the passage came from the abbot's room or the guest room.

The only people in the house tonight who knew of this particular passage were a few servants, her uncle and her grandmother. She wouldn't put it past her grandmother to be up to some mischief. Two could play her game.

She debated releasing the pin that held the secret door in her room locked from her side, or if she should go into the hall and around the corner toward the long gallery. She didn't hear any other creaks coming from the secret passage, so she tiptoed to her bedroom door and carefully opened it.

An oil lamp burned, with the wick turned low, from a table at the end of the hall.

Ann crept out of her room, closing her door but not completely, so no click could be heard. She carefully went down the hall to where the 'T' intersection of the adjoining hall led to the long gallery and the three entrances to the monastery. At the corner, she stopped to listen. She heard slight sounds coming from the guest room and the glow of candlelight from the partially opened door. What was grandmother up to? Hiding the sketches in the passage?

She crept closer to the door, but did not go in. When her grandmother came out, she wanted to surprise her. She used to worry that giving her grandmother a surprise might cause apoplexy. Now she didn't. She swore her grandmother thrived on surprise. She grinned. She'd forgotten how fun it could be to be a part of grandmother's roguery.

She heard a bump against furniture, then soft swearing. It was a man's voice! This was not her grandmother's game! Ann felt her chest tighten.

Whoever it was, they were coming toward the door. She picked up the vase of flowers from the table near her. She held it as high as she could, ready to throw despite its weight.

Ann recognized the man when he came out the door carrying a candlestick. She relaxed, lowering the vase a little. "Colonel Brantley!" she exclaimed in a whisper. "What are you doing?"

He pushed past her. Her trick knee gave out as she fell back against the wall. As she twisted, she tried to catch herself on the table. She was too over balanced. She, the table, and the vase crashed to the floor.

Searing pain clouded her mind. Startled, Ann lay still, assessing her situation. She heard voices and doors open from down the hall.

The table landed on her ankle. The vase broke. Water drenched her and the gigantic bouquet lay scattered across her and the floor. Her knee hurt, but she thought her ankle hurt worse. She tried to turn to sit up, but sharp pain accompanied movement, for the table trapped her leg. She pushed herself up on her side as best she could as she heard the voices coming to investigate the crash.

"Miss Hallowell!

"Ann!"

"Are you all right?"

"Let me help you up."

The last from the Marquis of Peverley.

"The table first," she got out, ignoring his outstretched hand. "It's trapped my ankle."

Miles lifted the table away from her. She took the Marquis's hand to rise.

"*Ow! No!*" she exclaimed, sagging back to the floor. At least now she could sit up. "I don't think I can stand," she said breathlessly. The sharp pain she'd felt as she started to rise quickly subsided to just pain; however, Ann didn't know whether to laugh or cry.

"*What's going on? What happened?*"

It was her grandmother coming from her suite.

"My bad knee collapsed, and I took the table with me as I fell," Ann said.

She didn't know why she didn't call out Colonel Brantley for his role in her mishap. She needed to think this through, away from the surrounding crowd.

"I think I've sprained my ankle," she said apologetically.

"And broken my Sèvres vase," her grandmother observed.

Ann nodded.

"That's two things broken this weekend," said the Duchess, frowning. "—Ellinbourne, please pick up my granddaughter and take her back to her room. It is just around the corner on the left."

"My pleasure," Miles said. He helped her stand on one leg, then bent down to pick her up.

Ann felt color suffuse her cheeks. Luckily it was night and dim in the hall.

"Lord Peverley, Lady Peverley, thank you for coming out. You can return to your room now. The servants will be up to clean up the mess. We'll see you in the morning," the Duchess said.

She led the way to Ann's bedroom and pulled the bell pull near the door.

"Can you hold her for a moment while I find a tinderbox to light a candle?"

"I am happy to," Miles said, and Ann felt her cheeks growing warmer.

"There is one on the mantle," Ann told her grandmother.

Her grandmother found it and quickly lit a candle which she took over to the oil lamp on the table to light that as well.

"Let's get her on her bed," the Duchess said, opening the heavy drapes.

Miles came past her to carefully lay Ann down.

"This is so embarrassing," Ann said, too aware how the water from the vase made her nightrail and wrapper cling to her body.

"What happened?" her grandmother asked, clasping her hands before her.

Miles moved to leave; however, the Duchess caught his arm as he would have passed her. He looked at her quizzically, but stayed where he was. The Duchess kept her attention on her granddaughter.

Ann sighed and leaned back. She pulled the corner of the quilt over her wet night clothes. "I heard a noise, like the creak of a floorboard coming from the passage."

"From here?" her grandmother asked, waving at the wall.

"Yes. I thought it might be you setting up some prank or another," Ann said.

Miles looked at the wall.

"I'd already put a locking pin in the door leading to the passage, so I didn't worry about anyone coming in here; but I thought if it were you, I could give you a surprise instead."

"You put a locking pin in this door? How did you

do that?" the Duchess asked, looking toward where she knew the hidden door was.

"I did that several years ago. I had one of the carpenter's apprentices drill a hole in the molding for me and I had the village blacksmith make a long metal pin that I could stick in through the door to the wall. I'm sure they could force it open, but that would make a lot of noise. I thought the pin was enough to deter any pranks the cousins might plan."

The Duchess clasped her hands together. "Clever girl! Well done! But continue your story about how you came to be out in the hall covered in water and flowers."

"As I said, I thought it was you. I saw a slight light coming from the guest bedroom that also leads to the passage. I stood outside the door, waiting for you to exit. Then I heard someone bump into something in the room and swear. It was a man's voice. I picked up the vase, but when the man came out, I thought it was Colonel Brantley."

"Brantley!" exclaimed Miles.

Ann nodded.

The Duchess frowned.

"It never occurred to me," Ann continued, "that the Colonel might do me harm or be up to some bit of nastiness. I started to put the vase down when he shoved me aside and ran down the hall. That is when my knee collapsed, and I fell, taking the table with me and making that monumental mess and unholy amount of noise. I am so sorry."

"Sorry! What have you to be sorry about?" her grandmother demanded. "If anyone should be sorry, it is me. I have not been taking this bizarre interest in these sketches seriously enough. Are you certain it was Colonel Brantley?"

"No. It was dark, but his size was the same. If not Colonel Brantley, then I suppose The Chicken comes closest to him in shape."

The Duchess chuckled. "I cannot get over you calling Sir Robert *The Chicken*."

The maid appeared in the doorway. "You rang, Your Grace?"

"Yes, Donna, my granddaughter has met with an accident walking around at night. There is broken glass, flowers, and water in the hall. Could you take care of that, please?"

The maid curtsied. "Yes, Your Grace."

"Do you want me to notify Mr. Martin?" Miles asked the Duchess.

She nodded. "I think that would be best. And my son as well. This room has a private parlor to the right. Ask them to come there."

"May I be present to learn what is going on?"

"I insist!"

Miles inclined his head and went to wake Nowlton and Mr. Martin.

LEWIS MARTIN ENTERED the small parlor bearing a tray with glasses and a sherry decanter. "I thought you and Miss Hallowell might need this," Lewis told the Duchess.

The Duchess chuckled slightly. "You have embraced your footman role."

"I have certainly learned a great deal," he said. He set the tray down and poured a bit of sherry into glasses for the Duchess and Ann.

"Thank you," Ann said. "This is perfect."

When Ellinbourne left to get Nowlton and Mr.

Martin, Ann used the time to get on dry clothing. Leaning heavily on her grandmother, she'd hobbled and winced her way into her parlor, where she collapsed on the small settee. The sherry was exceedingly welcome by then.

"Gentleman?" Lewis asked, turning to Miles and Nowlton.

They nodded and Lewis poured them and himself sherry. He sat down and pulled out his occurrence book and a pencil from his hastily donned clothes.

"I heard from His Grace the story of what happened. I won't make you repeat the entire thing, but I have a few questions."

"I'll try to answer as well as I may," Ann promised. She took a sip of sherry. Her ankle throbbed. They had wrapped her foot and elevated it, but it ached. She would be happy to go back to sleep. They might tempt her with a bit of laudanum if the throbbing did not subside any.

"What woke you?" Lewis asked.

"The squeak of a floorboard."

His brow furrowed. "How many times did you hear this squeak?"

"Twice. When it woke me up and when I sat up in bed listening before I got up."

He looked up from his notebook. "How many entrances or exits does this passage have?"

"I only know of three. Nowlton? Grandmother?" she asked, looking between her uncle and her grandmother.

"Just three," the Duchess said. "The one from Ann's bedroom, the one from the guest bedroom, and the one from the abbot's office.

"Is there anything special about that passage? It

seems odd to have a passage like that without an outside exit."

"That was a question that many of my husband's ancestors had. There is an area of cupboards in the passage at the long gallery end, which was discovered in 1662. It was full of ecclesiastical items. Some items had a handsome value, like gold communion goblets and the jeweled head of a Bishop's staff," the Duchess explained. "But, in total, it wasn't particularly noteworthy treasure. The family *treasure* rumored to be here wasn't discovered until forty years later. It was in a niche hidden behind a particularly hideous family portrait tucked away in a corner of the east gallery. It also wasn't an outrageous amount, but enough for the family to make improvements to the property and return it to profitability. That discovery didn't occur until 1701."

"Then I discovered more church items four years ago, and rumors started that there was more treasure to be found here," Ann added.

"So, you think someone was looking for treasure?" Lewis asked.

"No, not really, but it should be noted as a possibility, don't you think?"

Lewis grinned. "I'm a Bow Street agent. I consider all possibilities, that's why I asked to get a feeling for your perception of likelihood. But back to the events. Why did you go out into the hall and not into the passage?"

"While I thought it was my grandmother, I didn't want to give away my knowledge to her. To open that door in my room would have made noise as I installed a locking pin several years ago. I couldn't have removed it silently. And I thought I might surprise grandmother in turn by being outside in the hall expecting her."

"But you didn't know which door she would use."

"No, I didn't; however, I saw the guest bedroom door ajar and there was a candle glow from inside. That decided me. I waited outside that bedroom, happily anticipating surprising grandmother.—As children, that was the pinnacle of a youthful visit if one of us could manage to surprise grandmother. We rarely did."

"Oh, you troublemakers did more than you think. I just was able to hide it," her grandmother said, winking at her.

Ann laughed. "Now you tell me." She turned back to Mr. Martin. "When I heard a thump from in the room and heard a man's voice swear, I was suddenly afraid. I didn't have time to turn and run back to my room. I picked up the vase of fresh flowers from the table and held it up, ready to throw it. But when the man came out, he looked like Colonel Brantley. I relaxed then. Of course, there would be a good reason for his being there, that crossed my thoughts. But when I said his name, he ran past me and pushed me against the wall."

"Deliberately?"

"I don't know. But I have a trick knee, so when I was put off balance I couldn't recover. My knee collapsed. I dropped the vase as I twisted around to try to catch myself as I fell. I took the table with me, smashed grandmother's vase, and had water and flowers everywhere. Whoever the man was, he had to have heard me fall, but he did not return to help or see what happened."

Lewis frowned as he tapped his pencil against his occurrence book. He looked up. "What do you know about Colonel Brantley?" he asked, looking at the others in the room.

"He's my stepmother's suitor. She met him six months ago at some event. I don't know which one as I don't attend all that she does. She likes parties."

"He is quite a bit older than her," he observed.

"Yes, but so was my father. She feels more comfortable with an older man," Ann explained.

Lewis nodded, then looked at the Duchess and Nowlton. They both shook their heads.

"I believe he was attached to the Home Office at one time," Nowlton said.

"Yes! I think that is right. During the carriage journey here, he seemed to get uncomfortable when the subject of spying and spies came up," Ann said.

"Particularly the mention of Harry Blessingame and the rumor of him being a spy," Miles offered.

"Yes, Colonel Brantley quickly changed the subject."

"Ann, you should tell Mr. Martin what you overheard this afternoon."

"Oh! This afternoon! How could I have forgotten? Yes. I meant to speak to you, but there never seemed to be an opportunity."

"When and where did this occur? And between whom?"

"I was in the library. There were two men outside the library. It sounded like they came from the direction of the estate room. The first man I am certain was Colonel Brantley. He asked the second man if he had learned anything. The second man said no and asked Colonel Brantley if he had. He said no as well, and Colonel Brantley swore angrily that nothing was learned. Then the second man asked Brantley what he thought of the head footman. Brantley said nothing, that he was just trying to curry favor with the Duchess and was too full of himself.

Lewis laughed.

"Laugh, yes, but the second man said something struck him as *off* about you. Said you were too intelligent for a footman role."

"I don't know if I should be pleased, or disappointed. Disappointed that my playacting isn't better, or pleased that they can see me as an intelligent man."

"Who was the second man?"

"I don't know. I thought it might be the Marquis. His voice was indistinct so I couldn't tell, and my angle where I sat prevented me from seeing the gentlemen."

Lewis rose from his seat and began pacing the room.

"We know Colonel Brantley is trying to *learn* something, probably not trying to take something—though I won't rule that out either. The question is what."

"I have never seen those two together," said the Duchess.

"That could be on purpose," Nowlton suggested.

"Let's focus on Peverley for a moment, like we did Colonel Brantley," Lewis said. "What do you know of him?"

"He began collecting seriously about five years ago, about the time he married," Nowlton said.

"Did his wife bring him a large dowry?" Lewis asked.

"Yes, but he didn't need it. His fortune was large enough."

"Was his wife interested in art and pushed him in that direction?"

Nowlton thought for a moment. "No-o-o," he said

slowly. "His wife is the former Miss Margaret Chill-inghurst."

"Political family, always danced in Castlereagh's orbit," the Duchess explained. "She was no young debutante when they married, either." Her eyes narrowed as she thought back. "That was about the time I was withdrawing from London activities, so I wasn't paying a lot of attention to society drama. I think Margaret acted as hostess for her brother until he unexpectedly decided to wed, and her services were no longer needed."

"Yes, that's right," said Nowlton. "Rumored to be a marriage of convenience for both of them. No children yet. They travel a great deal—did so even while Boney was at large making mischief for Wellington. They were at the Congress of Vienna, too."

"The Congress of Vienna? What would take them there?"

"That was another location to buy art cheap, as was suggested by Lady Travis.

"So, Brantley is of a political bent while Peverley is of a collector bent—though his wife is political. Has anyone seen her talking to Colonel Brantley?"

No one had.

Lewis paced the room.

"I think it was Peverley you heard, Miss Hallowell. The hair on my back of my neck tingles. Laugh if you will. That's a sign I'm on the correct path in my thinking."

"I wouldn't laugh, Mr. Martin. It is your profession to perceive relationships others may not."

"I don't think anything more will be resolved tonight," said the Duchess. "We should all return to our beds. Ellinbourne, Aidan, assist Ann back into the other room if you would please. Mr. Martin, I suggest an examination of the passage in the morning."

"Very good, Your Grace."

Nowlton and Miles made a chair with their crossed arms to carry Ann back to her bed.

"I'll have the butler find your old bath chair from the attic, Ann," her grandmother said.

Ann made a face. "Must I?"

"Yes, unless you choose to be relegated to your room until your ankle recovers."

Ann nodded ruefully. "Very well.

The Duchess picked up the branch of candles and led everyone out of the parlor.

CHAPTER 14
THE VISCOUNT

The next morning all during breakfast the guests talked of nothing but Miss Hallowell hearing someone in the secret passage—which everyone voiced a desire to visit—then catching someone coming out of the empty guest room.

The Marquis was the bearer of the tale to the guests as he and the Marchioness were there, as were Miles and the Duchess, who all had rooms in the vicinity and heard the crash, he told the others.

"Thought I heard something last night," Lord Druffner said.

"Druffner!" Lady Druffner exclaimed, slapping her husband's arm with her napkin. "How could you not wake me? We missed everything," she said, quite dismayed.

"Took it for some servant catastrophe. Best to ignore such things. I turned over and went back to sleep."

"Oh!" his wife exclaimed. She sighed deeply.

"Poor girl was on the floor when we came out of our room," Peverley said. "Knocked the table over on herself. Broke the vase. Water and flowers strewn everywhere."

"Was she hurt?" asked Lord Wolfred.

"Sprained her ankle," Miles said over the rim of his coffee cup.

"Two accidents. Two people hurt," intoned Lady Druffner.

"Did she see anyone?" Colonel Brantley asked.

Miles shook his head. "Just said it was a large man. Said she thought it was you at first, but realized it wasn't when the man shoved her aside and did not come to her aid when she fell."

"Me?"

Miles nodded. "Had your build."

"Brantley," Nowlton said. "Ellinbourne and I were discussing this earlier. We know you worked for the Home Office. Would you mind coming to the estate office after breakfast with us? You can give us ideas as to how to properly investigate this. We are from the art world. This is foreign to us."

"I should be happy to," Brantley said, lifting his head proudly, his chin leading.

Miles stared at him. Ann professed confidence it was Brantley who came out of that room. If that was the case, it was obvious Colonel Brantley was an able dissembler.

An image of punching that leading chin flashed into Miles' mind.

"It is so good of you to help," cooed Mrs. Hallowell, looking up at Colonel Brantley as if the sun rose and set with him.

Miles looked down.

~

"THANK YOU FOR HELPING US," Nowlton told Colonel Brantley as they sat down around a worn and mellowed old oak table used for spreading out drawings of the home farms, the upcoming planting season plans, and estate repairs.

"Of course, of course," Brantley said, leaning back in his chair.

"Are you aware of the threats the Duchess has been receiving the last few weeks?" Nowlton asked.

"Threats?" Brantley repeated. "No, what kind of threats?"

"She has been directed to sell the Michelangelo sketches in their frames. Veiled threats of harm to her family have been made, the implied consequences of not selling."

"Who is she to sell them to?"

Nowlton shrugged. "We don't know. There has been no suggestion of a buyer. And the last missive said time is running out."

"Why doesn't she sell the sketches, then?"

Nowlton stared at the man a moment, then laughed. "Really, you ask that?" he said. "My mother hardly ever did what my father wanted, let alone what anyone else might want her to do."

The Colonel looked perturbed. "She has always been known to be eccentric, but I hardly would have guessed she would be this mad."

"I can assure you, Colonel, my mother is not mad. Are you suggesting she succumb to blackmail?" Nowlton asked.

"To jeopardize her own life and the lives of her family—" Brantley protested.

"How can we be sure this is a significant threat?" Nowlton asked.

"You can't, but you can't be sure it isn't either.

Someone did not plan their strategy well. Quite surprising," he mused, frowning.

Miles thought that last hinted at knowledge. "Surprising? How so?" he asked.

Brantley shook his head. "Just overall," he said. "But I do have an idea," he said, leaning forward and planting his hands on the table. "Why don't you sell them to me?" he suggested. "Not actually, but we could pretend. I could keep the pictures for a while, then quietly return them to the Duchess in a month or so."

Miles looked at Nowlton. This was not a scenario they had considered as they discussed this meeting earlier.

Nowlton's mobile left eyebrow climbed his brow in the peculiar habit he had. He looked over at Miles.

Miles lifted one hand slightly.

Nowlton looked at Colonel Brantley. "What you are suggesting has considerable merit; however, that does not lead us to whomever was in the passage last night. That is a passage known only to family members and a few staff."

"Really? I would have thought it known—no matter," he said, shaking a beringed chubby hand. "If we obviate the threat to the Duchess and her family, doesn't that resolve the issue?" Colonel Brantley suggested.

"No," Nowlton responded. "Someone else has knowledge of the house's secrets. That puts my family in danger."

Colonel Brantley frowned, his brow furrowing.

"We can't be sure there won't be more threats in the future and quite frankly, just seeing the Michelangelo sketches in someone else's hands as an end to the danger makes no sense," Nowlton continued. "That's like a prank my mother would think up and I assure you, she is not the author of this situation. She is definitely concerned."

That's like a prank my mother would think up.

The phrase rang church bells in Mile's head. Could it be a prank any of her extended family would think up? An ultimate revenge for being on the receiving end of pranks for years?

But if it was a prank, why bash in Mr. Holbein's head? What did he have to do with a lifetime of pranks? And why was Colonel Brantley in the hidden passage in the dead of night?

There were more questions than answers.

AFTER ENJOYING breakfast in her room, Ann requested Lucy to get two footmen to help her downstairs. To her consternation, someone had retrieved her old Bath wheelchair from the attic and already put it in the parlor.

"Please take me to the sofa," Ann directed when they would have placed her in the wheeled chair.

"Why don't you sit in the Bath chair?" asked her grandmother, following them into the room. "I had it cleaned and brought down for you."

"That has got to be one of the most uncomfortable chairs I have ever sat it. I swear it is a torture device, not a helping device," Ann said.

Her grandmother laughed. She sat down in the chair at right angles to the sofa and next to the Bath chair. "What do you mean? It has a nice cane seat and back," she said, running her hand over the smooth, bent wood arm.

"Yes, it does, but look at the angle of the chair

back. It is much too straight. And a pillow at my back only pitches me forward. I learned that with my knee injury. This was an ill-designed chair, and I was happy to stop sitting in it. My injury is not so bad this time that I require this contraption again. Where are my crutches? Those would work fine."

"I gave them to one of the tenant farm families when their oldest broke his leg."

Ann made a face. "I admit that was a splendid notion. All right, I will use this to go from room to room down here, but I will not sit in it any longer than needful."

"Thank you. I really did not want to have a couple of footmen come to carry you around everywhere," the Duchess said archly. She grabbed a large shawl from off the back of the sofa and spread it across the Ann's legs.

Ann wrinkled her nose in response. "If anyone had thought to come upstairs to tell me what is going on, I would not have had to come downstairs, now would I?"

"Oh! My kitten has claws," her grandmother said.

"I learned from the best."

Her grandmother nodded. "I taught you well, didn't I."

They heard a flurry of sounds from the front entrance. Ann leaned to the side to see into the hall. A young man wearing a cloak with multiple capes stood just inside the door. He had one arm in a sling and one eye sported a deep purple shiner.

Redinger

"Where is she?" he demanded of their butler. He tossed his hat to the man and worked at the gloved fingers to remove his gloves one-handed.

"Miss Hallowell is in the parlor," Botsford intoned.

"Not her, you nimrod. Miss Quesinberry! Where is Julia Quesinberry? Miles said she was here!"

"Miss Quesinberry is touring the galleries with the other guests," they heard their butler say repressively.

The Duchess laid her finger to her lips, then motioned to Ann that she would leave the parlor by the terrace door.

Ann looked at her quizzically and spread her hands out to silently ask why.

The Duchess pantomimed entering through another door and going upstairs to get Miss Quesinberry.

"Mr. Botsford," called out Ann as her grandmother left. "Escort him in here, please."

"But I don't want to go in there. I want to find my Juliet!" whined Redinger.

Ann decided his accident was fortuitous for her. A grown man whining?

"Please, my lord, this way," said a pained Botsford.

Redinger allowed himself to be led into the parlor, though he stopped every few steps to look over his shoulder.

"Please come in, my Lord," Ann said. "I'm afraid I'm stuck on this sofa for the moment and cannot reach the bell pull. If you would please pull it for me? —Yes, thank you. You must be parched from your fast travel to get here so early in the day from London."

"Miss Hallowell?" Redinger asked as he approached her.

She saw him frown and stare at her chin. It was all she could do not to touch her scar.

"Yes, and you are Viscount Redinger. I know we have not been formally introduced, but under the circumstances we can put that aside, don't you agree?"

"What? Oh, yes, yes. Totally agree."

She smiled at him. "Please be seated and the staff will find Miss Quesinberry and escort her here. She will be as delighted to see you as you appear to be delighted at the prospect of seeing her."

"Yes! She is my heart! My joy!" Redinger said rapturously.

Ann half smiled. "Yet you would have wed me," she said.

He shrugged. "I thought never to see my Juliet again and I do have a duty."

Ann squirmed inwardly again at the knowledge she would have been a make-do wife. But she smiled at him anyway.

"What happened between you?" she asked.

Redinger frowned. "I don't know. We'd made plans to meet again, but she never showed and later I received a note from her that said she considered herself too far beneath me to continue our relationship. Beneath me! That's a lark! I am so far beneath her I don't deserve to walk the same earth or breathe the same air!" he cried out.

Ann smiled and nodded, suppressing a laugh. "I understand," she said solemnly, though she thought his hyperbole a bit tedious. "After talking to Miss Quesinberry I can say with confidence that note you received was a forgery."

"Forgery?"

"Yes, she never wrote such a piece, just as I am certain that you never sent your butler to her home to inform her and her mother that you had reconsidered the connection."

"What? Randolph?"

Miles walked into the room. "Yes, the efficient, loyal Randolph."

"Never. Not Randolph," Redinger denied. "He has been with me since I set up my own household."

"Where was he before he worked for you?" Miles asked.

"He was the head footman at my father's estate. Father said he saw promise in the man and encouraged me to take him on. I did and haven't regretted it. It makes no sense for him to put a spoke in my wheel. Why would he do that?" Redinger asked. He shifted his sling up on his shoulder.

Miles shrugged. "I don't know. My guess is his loyalty does not lie with you, but with your father."

"With my..." Redinger's eyes widened, then he frowned. "He did write to my parents to inform them of my accident without my instruction to do so. But why would my parents object to Miss Quesinberry? She comes from a good family and has a good dowry."

"Did you tell Randolph any of that?" Ann asked.

"Egad, no," he said dismissively. "Man's my butler."

"My guess is he assumed the worse of the Quesinberrys and thought to curry favor with your parents by putting a stop to the relationship before they learned of it. I wouldn't be surprised if he has kept them informed of your other activities as well."

"Like the incident with the damned watch," Redinger groused.

"Sebastian?"

It was Julia Quesinberry. They heard her feet running across the marble hall floor.

Sebastian stood up. "Juliet!" he called, moving as if in a daze toward the open door.

Miles and Ann exchanged glances.

Julia appeared at the door. When she saw Sebastian, she gave a little cry and rushed into his arms.

He winced at the force of her embrace. Julia stepped back.

"Oh! You *are* hurt. They told me—" She broke off, her hands lightly touching the bruises on his face, his arm in a sling. "Oh, Sebastian!" She started to cry.

Ann didn't know where to look. She felt like a voyeur.

At that moment, the Quesinberrys and the Duchess entered the parlor.

"Oh, Mama! Look! It is Sebastian, and he's been hurt."

"I am glad to see you, my lord, and happy that you were not the author of that terrible missive to my daughter."

"No, Mrs. Quesinberry," Sebastian said earnestly. He looked back at Julia. "Never. I love my Juliet."

Mr. Quesinberry cleared his throat.

Julia flushed bright pink into the curls of her red hair. She stepped away from Sebastian but took his hand in hers and led him to her father. "Father, this is Sebastian Redinger, Viscount Redinger. Sebastian, this is my father, Mr. Hadley Quesinberry."

Sebastian squared his shoulders. "It appears we have both been led astray. I should like to have a word with you in private, sir."

"Oh, very good, very good, Lord Redinger," said the Duchess, clapping her hands together. "Why don't you two go into the library for a nice discussion."

"But—" Sebastian started to protest.

"I understand. You have just found each other again. Best get over heavy ground as quickly as possible. Then you can all go to see the archbishop this afternoon about a special license."

"Special License!" protested Mr. Quesinberry.

"Of course. Ellinbourne sent the Galboroughs a

letter yesterday informing them of the situation between Miss Quesinberry and the Viscount. I expect
them to be here by end of day. Best if you are all gone
together to get the special license and see they are wed
as soon as possible. These two have had needless suffering, so it is up to us to see to their happiness as soon
as possible."

"But if you think the Galboroughs would object—"
began Mr. Quesinberry.

"No, no, not object. But drag everything on inter-
minably and be determined to manage everything as
well. They would want their solicitors involved and
want promises from your brother, all manner of med-
dlesome activities. These two would be lucky to be
married before year end."

Mr. Quesinberry frowned. "I believe Truett, Trout,
and Pendergast are his solicitors. They are more about
pandering to their aristocratic clients than they are
about following the law."

"Then you know my concern. Now, off with you to
your gentlemanly talks. You can probably use what
you drew up for Ann and Redinger as your basis for
discussion. It will go much quicker," said the
Duchess.

Mr. Quesinberry nodded slowly. "All right. Come,
my lord, let's do as the Duchess suggests," he said,
walking to the door.

Sebastian looked back longingly at Julia, then followed her father.

"Mrs. Quesinberry, I suggest you and Miss Quesinberry go upstairs and see that your things are packed
and ready for a departure."

Julia ran up to the Duchess and grabbed her hand.
"Thank you! Oh, thank you so much, Your Grace!" She
ran out of the room ahead of her mother.

"You believe this is for the best?" Mrs. Quesinberry asked the Duchess.

The Duchess sighed. "I do. The Galboroughs have the best of intentions; however, they are managing people. It is their nature."

"All right then. Thank you for your hospitality, as brief as it has been," said Mrs. Quesinberry.

"You're quite welcome."

"Well done, grandmother!" Ann said after Mrs. Quesinberry had left.

"An expert bit of maneuvering," said Miles. "Wellington could have used you."

"Or better yet, Uncle Candelstone," Ann said. "Maybe he wouldn't have had to retire if you'd been helping him."

Her grandmother laughed. "I didn't want to give them time to think it through," she said. "Excuse me, to further their departure, I will make arrangements for them to leave in my traveling chaise," she said with her conspiratorial smile. She left the parlor.

"Has Mr. Martin had his discussion with Colonel Brantley yet?" Ann asked the Duke. "I've been wondering all morning, and no one has come to tell me anything. That is why I had the footmen help me downstairs."

"Not Mr. Martin, directly, as he thought it best, he maintain his footman role a while longer. He coached Nowlton and I. We requested Colonel Brantley join us in the estate room after breakfast as it has a ledger closet that Mr. Martin could hide in to listen to everything. Colonel Brantley denied everything. Acted quite taken back and hurt by the accusation. Claimed you were mistaken. He suggested you hit your head when you fell, Ann."

"How would he know I fell unless he was there?"

"Unfortunately, that was the talk all through breakfast. He couldn't help but learn of it."

Ann made a moue. Miles thought the pouty lip was quite enchanting.

"So where does that leave us?" Ann asked.

"I don't know," said Miles, sitting in the chair the Duchess vacated. "Colonel Brantley suggested he do a mock purchase of the sketches, since whoever is threatening your grandmother only wants the sketches out of her hands."

"This does not make any sense!" Ann exclaimed.

"Colonel Brantley did say something that I took note of. He said someone did not plan their strategy well. Then he said, *Quite surprising*. And the way he said that led me to think he might know who is behind this, but won't say."

"Poor Ursula," Ann said. "I fear it looks like he has some involvement and if that is true, she will be without a suitor."

"Why do you say that?"

"Ursula may seem flighty; however, the woman is as loyal as they come. She would not countenance being used, as Colonel Brantley might be doing, to get closer to the family."

"We don't know enough yet to make rash decisions on courses of action," Miles warned.

"True. But how are we to learn more?"

"Mr. Martin has sent inquires to London about Colonel Brantley. In the meantime, we must keep a close eye on him."

Ann nodded, but she no longer felt comfortable with him squiring her stepmother about.

CHAPTER 15

AN ABBEY OUTING

"Have you gentleman come to an agreement?" the Duchess asked Lord Redinger and Mr. Quesinberry when they came out of the library an hour later.

"Yes, perfect agreement," said Mr. Quesinberry. "I had written up the settlement you had asked me for earlier with a mind as to what I would want for my daughter, so there wasn't much to change."

"And you, Lord Redinger, are you happy with the terms?"

"Terms don't matter, only my Juliet matters," he said with a sigh.

Mr. Quesinberry smiled indulgently at him. "He has been like this the entire time. He would sign away his life if I'd put that on a piece of paper. I watched out for the lad. Odd to be on both sides, but it is for family."

"Exactly. Very well done. Now, I've put my traveling chaise and coachman at your disposal," the Duchess told them. "And I've written a letter for the archbishop telling him of my approval of the match and request that he expedite matters for you." She handed the letter to Mr. Quesinberry.

"Make sure this gets into the archbishop's hands and not just handed over to a clerk. Those prelate clerks are overly protective of their superiors. One must sometimes speak quite firmly with them. They feel they have God on their side, you see. Well, I suppose they do, but not in preventing communication with the archbishop."

"I've requested fresh horses from the inn in the village for your servants' carriage," the Duchess continued. "They won't be far behind you. Oh, this is so exciting!" said the Duchess. "Don't you think so, Ann?" she asked, turning toward her granddaughter.

"Yes, very exciting," Ann agreed calmly from where she reclined on the sofa with her foot propped up.

She'd stayed with her grandmother when she returned from ordering her carriage and while they waited for the gentlemen to complete their business— not that she had any place to go as she hated the wheeled chair. The Duke said he, Nowlton, and Mr. Martin were going to inspect the passage. She felt intensely jealous at not being part of their investigations.

As they waited, her grandmother told her she wanted to make sure she hurried Viscount Redinger and the Quesinberrys on their way without them having the time to think of any reason why they should prolong their stay. The Earl would twist it up in legalities. That just would not do.

Soon the wedding party was on their way, Miss Quesinberry wringing Ann's hand, saying how noble she was to forego a marriage with Sebastian, but she did love him so.

"I believe you. Now, be off. Let him take you away."

"Yes. Thank you again. Thank you, Your Grace. I'm so happy!" the young woman said, fairly bouncing on her toes.

The Duchess gently put her hand on the young woman's back and steered her toward the parlor door. "You're quite welcome. Now off you go," she said as the group was in the hall. John had the front door open and waiting for them to leave.

More thank yous were given before they were finally out the door and on their way to the carriage.

"Goodbye!" the Duchess called out to them. She turned to John. "Go out there and make sure they all get in the carriage and leave as soon as possible. No forgetting something or more delays. Their servants can bring anything they think they forgot."

John bowed. "Yes, Your Grace." He went out the door after them, pulling the door closed behind him.

Ann watched her grandmother through the open parlor door.

"You look pleased with yourself," she said when her grandmother returned to the parlor.

"I am." She made a face. "I'm not fond of Winsted, so putting any spike in his plans is great fun." She sat down in one of the wing chairs.

"Winsted?"

"Viscount Redinger's father, the Earl of Galborough. He, and his father before him, were cronies of your grandfather's when he attended sessions of parliament. Bertram would insist he be invited to all our social events. When Winsted came, all he did was complain! Quite maddening."

"You never played a prank on him?"

"I never pranked any of your grandfather's political cronies. They were all like him, quite staid. I loved your grandfather to distraction; however, he could not understand fun. In many ways, Arthur is like him and why I do not like Aidan belittling his brother. Arthur came by his serious nature from his father, bless his soul."

"Excuse me, Your Grace."

The Duchess looked toward the door. "Yes, John?"

"Mr. Samuel Johnson, the estate carpenter, is here, your Grace."

"Mr. Johnson here? What is his business?" she asked.

"He made Miss Hallowell crutches."

"Crutches? And I didn't even request them. Bless his soul. Send him in, John."

Ann beamed at her grandmother. "This is excellent!"

"Indeed," said the Duchess.

A moment later, the door opened to admit a wiry older gentleman with salt and pepper hair and beard —more salt than pepper—carrying a set of crutches.

"G'day, Yur Grace. I heard as how the young Miss done hurt herself agin and be needful of crutches, so I fashioned her a new pair."

"Bless you, Mr. Johnson," enthused the Duchess.

Ann threw the shawl off of her legs and swung her feet to the floor. "You are a savior, Mr. Johnson."

"Gots to see how they fit," said the man. "Can I—" he held out the crutches toward Ann, silently asking if he could cross the room to give them to her.

"Of course!" said the Duchess.

The man rocked his way to Ann on legs bowed with age and arthritis. He handed one crutch to Ann, who immediately used it to pull herself up. Balanced on one foot, she took the second crutch from him and tucked them under her arms.

"They're perfect!" She exclaimed. "How did you get them to be the right height? I remember we had trouble getting them right five years ago."

"Mrs. Weaver said as how she thought Ellie, the dairy maid, was your height. Ellie worked with me to get them right."

"Mrs. Weaver was correct! These are perfect!"

The crutches had the hand holds wrapped in soft leather and the part that went under her arms was covered in padded sheep skin. Ann held up her bad foot and hobbled across the room and back with her crutches.

"Thank you, Mr. Johnson," the Duchess said, watching Ann maneuver around the furniture. My granddaughter is not one for sitting around. These are a great boon. You will not be forgotten."

The man nodded, embarrassed. "Thank ye." He rocked back out of the room.

"Where are the men?" Ann asked her grandmother.

"The men?"

Ann rolled her eyes. Her lips quirked into a wry smile. "None of that, Grandmother. Where are Nowlton, the Duke, and Mr. Martin? What are they doing? Are they still exploring that passage? What else has been happening since last night? And, now that I think of it, where is Lady Oakley and what have you sent her to do?" Ann asked, realizing that Lady Oakley had been everywhere except by her grandmother. As those women had been friends since school days, Ann didn't trust them not to be plotting something.

"Lady Oakley is making friends," declared the Duchess.

"*Uh huh,*" said Ann. "Making friends with a purpose, I'll warrant. You are incorrigible!"

The Duchess shrugged. "No one pays attention to old, widowed women. We would make the best spies if that *almost gentleman's club* in London they refer to as *The Home Office* would open their eyes.—And your uncle's the worst of the lot. I have no idea how my own daughter can tolerate his insufferable arrogance. He believes he knows what is in the best interests for the country and acts accordingly."

The door to the parlor opened. Ursula came in with Colonel Brantley. Ann found herself looking away from him immediately. She schooled her expression to open friendliness, surprised at the effort it took. Unconsciously, her mind and body recoiled seeing him.

"Oh! You're up! You have crutches!" Ursula said. "And here I am, coming to see if you needed me to bring you anything. The staff is setting out nuncheon in the dining room for any who want something," Ursula said.

"How kind of you, Ursula," Ann said, "but as you can see, I do have mobility now, so I will take myself into the dining room. I am done with sitting!"

Her stepmother laughed. "That doesn't surprise me. Well, come along then. The horde has already descended on the food. We shall be lucky for a crumb."

Ann waited for her grandmother to stand and start walking to the dining room. She stayed close to her, paying attention to obstacles in her path as she maneuvered her crutches.

"Miss Hallowell," said Colonel Brantley from her left side. Ann looked up, surprised to find him next to her while her stepmother walked on with her grandmother to the dining room.

"I heard you thought I was the person who came

out of the hidden passage and knocked you down in the hall."

Ann looked away from him, concentrating on her crutches. "It was a man of your stature, Colonel Brantley. Surprised as I was, my first reaction was to believe it was you," she said evenly.

"I see. You do know now it wasn't, don't you." He made it a statement, not a question.

"I have discussed the darkness and the strange light a candle throws in that situation with my grandmother and uncle," she said, not directly answering him.

"Good, good." He barked a short, strained laugh. "I was asleep. I didn't learn anything until I came down to breakfast."

"Yes. And you don't sleepwalk," Ann said sweetly, sliding a glance at him.

"Sleepwalk! No!" He pulled a handkerchief out of his waistcoat and mopped his brow. "Do people actually do that?"

"My great-grandmother did. You should ask my uncle about that sometime."

He stepped back to let her pass through the dining room door first. Ann hurriedly went ahead and procured the help of the footman on duty to fill her plate for her and turned to find a seat between Lord Druffner and the Marquis of Peverley.

Ann was astounded that Colonel Brantley had approached her. And more astounded to see his nervousness. Now she felt certain it was Colonel Brantley who had pushed her aside, but it wouldn't serve anyone for her to accuse him. She narrowed her eyes as she watched him fill his plate. What had he been intent on *learning* in the passage, and how did he learn of the passage to begin with?

She caught her grandmother's questioning eye from her end of the table. Ann shrugged slightly and began to eat.

The Duchess smiled at her guests. "I'm sorry if I seemed to abandon you this morning. There were issues I needed to see to. The Quesinberrys who I introduced last evening encountered an emergency and decided it would be best if they left immediately to handle the issue. I helped them make the appropriate arrangements."

"But I am free this afternoon. Since it is a splendid day, we will walk through the old, ruined part of the abbey."

"Is it safe?" asked Lady Druffner

"Yes. I've had masons reinforce whichever walls looked weak and near to collapse. I quite like the ruin. It is a draw for visitors."

"Peasants," growled Lord Druffner, "Always traipsing about their better's properties."

The Duchess laughed. The Druffners were known for living on the largess of others. "How many estates have you visited since Yuletide?"

Red crept up Lord Druffner's neck. "I don't remember. What difference does that make?"

"It's been seven," supplied Lady Druffner cheerfully. "And they have been delightful visits. Except for Baron Dolhome," she added thoughtfully. "He asked us to leave after only two weeks. How rude."

"Mary!" admonished her husband.

"What?" she asked.

Ann raised her napkin to her lips to hide her laugher. She saw Mrs. Morrison do the same. Others looked pointedly at Lord Druffner.

Lord Druffner harrumphed and looked down at his plate, studiously shoveling food into his mouth.

Ann wondered if her grandmother would get to the point where she asked them to leave. Lady Druffner was nice; however, Lord Druffner was nosey, listening and prying where he didn't belong.

"Any bread and cheese left?" Nowlton asked as he and Ellinbourne came into the dining room.

"If not, John or Lewis can fetch more," the Duchess said. She looked them up and down. "Where have you two been?" she asked. Dust streaked their clothes.

"Beg pardon. We have been investigating the passage to see if the miscreant who attacked Ann left any clues behind," Nowlton said.

"It looks like they might have entered through the Abbot's room for the door there is not fully closed," Ellinbourne said. "You have some interesting pieces stashed in there. Are they for your expanded museum?"

The Duchess nodded. "That is my intention. There are also some Roman statues I think I'll put in the area of the ruin."

"We saw them. Covered in Holland covers? Correct?"

"Yes."

"Any large canvases like your cousin is looking for?" Ann asked as the men walked to the buffet.

Miles looked back over his shoulder. "No, but I'll confess I looked."

"What painting were you looking for?" asked the Duchess.

"A painting of the Earl of Norwalk," Miles told her.

The Duchess shook her head. "I don't know why you would think I would have the Earl of Norwalk's painting."

He shrugged. "I knew you had some Clarence

Wingate paintings, and the painting is from the Earl's youth." He brought his nuncheon snacks over to the table and sat down.

Ann was amused to note he didn't provide hints as to why he and his cousin were interested in the painting.

"I didn't think Wingate did portraits," the Marquis of Peverley said.

Miles nodded. "As a rule, that is true; however, with family there are some exceptions, and he did commission portraits when he was particularly low on funds, but they weren't his favorite subjects."

"Do you still paint?" the Marchioness asked.

He nodded as he chewed on a hunk of bread. "I have a painting in the Royal Academy of Arts spring show."

"That's where I've met you before!" declared Lord Wolfred.

"Yes," Miles admitted.

Ann saw the tension in his body as they questioned him about his painting and being at the Royal Academy of Art.

"We should talk about having your work at my gallery," said Nowlton.

Miles looked at him in surprise. "I'd like that. Yes."

Nowlton nodded. "When next we're both in London, then."

"Definitely," Miles said. He looked across the table at Ann, his expression bemused.

She smiled encouragingly back. Right then she would have hugged her uncle if she'd been mobile, and they not surrounded by others. Miles Wingate was a gifted artist—Duke or not.

She pushed her chair back. The footman hurried forward with her crutches. "If we are going to the abbey ruin, I need to have my maid fetch me a bonnet."

"If you insist on going, you will go in the wheeled chair," declared her grandmother. "Lewis will push you."

Ann wanted to complain about the chair but realized it would be hard to walk over any rough ground with crutches. And to have Mr. Martin push her would keep him in the company of everyone to hear what they said. She nodded. "Thank you for offering his services."

Ann hobbled out of the room. She encountered Donna in the grand hall and requested she send Lucy to her in the gold parlor. She made her way back to the gold parlor and had just sat down when Lady Oakley came in.

"I thought I should find you in here," Lady Oakley said.

Ann chuckled lightly. "Not many other places for me to go on these crutches." She shrugged. "At least the swelling seems a bit better."

"A turned ankle must be rested lest it be a continued problem," Lady Oakley said as she walked to the chair nearest Ann and sat down.

"Sadly, I know. At least it is only a wretched ankle and not like the injury I had five years ago."

"How did that occur?"

"My horse balked at a jump, but my body didn't. I went over his head, and the low fence I meant him to jump."

"Gracious! You could have been killed."

"Yes, so I have been told. And my punishment for my foolheartiness is a trick knee and a scar on my face. You know, my ankle wouldn't have the injury it does now if my knee hadn't buckled when I was pushed aside."

"Now, now, that is not self pity I'm hearing, is it?"

Ann had the grace to shrug and half smile. She looked down. "Perhaps a little," she admitted.

"That will not do at all," declared Lady Oakley. "If anyone should be pitied, it should be me."

"You!" Ann laughed. "You are bamming me!"

"Hardly. What I have borne these last two days because of the friendship I have for the Duchess is extraordinary."

"And what is that?" Ann asked, amused.

"Taking Lord Druffner in hand, of course. Bearing him company and making sure he does not go where he shouldn't. The man is a snoop. He doesn't think anyone should have an ounce of privacy from him. It is no wonder Baron Dolhome asked him to leave. The Baron, you know, is an inventor, and an inventor does not want their inventions to be known until they are ready. And they are certainly not to be broadcast about, as I understand Lord Druffner did."

"Showing him all this attention, aren't you concerned that he would deem your home a place he would be welcome to live in for a time?"

"Concerned? More than concerned. Terrified! He has already suggested it for the rest of the season."

"No!"

"Oh yes. However, I have managed to fob him off by telling him my house is being remodeled, not fit for company."

"And is it?"

"Actually, just the ballroom is, but he does not need to know that. I was quite tired of all that Chinoise, with its gold and snarling dragons. Prinny has not given up on Oriental decor; however, I have. I was going to wait to remodel the grand stairway until the summer. If pressed, I may change my mind," Lady Oakley said archly.

"I do remember a ball at your home the year of my come out. Your decor dazzled me."

"It was a bit extravagant, which made it fun," confessed Lady Oakley. "I don't quite know what I want this time, but by the time I return home, all the Oriental will be gone and I can study the design ideas better."

A timid knock on the parlor door was followed by Lucy entering. "Excuse me, my lady," Lucy said, curtsying to Lady Oakley. She walked over to Ann. "I brung your bonnet and your drawing things, Miss."

"Thank you, Lucy! I did not think to ask for my art supplies before, and I know I would miss having them." She used her crutches to push herself to her feet.

"I should go get my bonnet as well," stated Lady Oakley, rising.

"Let me help you with yur bonnet." Lucy said as Lady Oakely left. She carefully placed the bonnet on Ann's head and tied the ribbons under her chin to the side.

"Thank you. Now can you hold the wheeled chair for me so I can sit in it?"

Lucy quickly went to the back of the chair, took Ann's crutches from her when she was ready and steadied the chair.

"Can you push me into the hall?" Ann asked. "We can leave the crutches there for when we get back."

"Yes, Miss." Lucy handed Ann back her crutches, then wheeled her into the hall.

Ann was surprised to see all the house party assembled. She would have thought a few would have cried off, like Sir Robert Renouf or the Peverleys; however, they were there. Mr. Martin took the crutches from her, then handed them over to John to put away safely for their return.

He wheeled her out the door. Outside, two groomsmen stood waiting to grab hold of either side of the chair to carry it and her down the steps.

Ann laughed delightedly. "This is so silly," she said.

Lewis came up behind her to take over the chair from the groomsmen.

"Thank you, Jem and Eddie," Ann called back to them as Lewis pushed her chair forward.

"As I have not been long at Versely Park, Miss Hallowell, can you recommend the smoothest ground to take you to the ruins? Lewis asked.

"I suggest we go along the side to the right. There is a smaller doorway on that side. This doorway in front of us, as you obviously have discerned, has too many crumbling fallen stones hidden in the taller grass."

"I did note that. Why is it not manicured, as the rest of the grounds are?"

Ann laughed. "Because that would take away from the romanticism of the ruin."

"Ah. I am not by nature a romantic. I tend more to the absolute."

"That comes from being with Bow Street, I imagine," she suggested as the wheeled chair bumped over the exposed roots of a large oak that spread its branches above them.

She tucked her art supplies next to her and gripped the arms of the chair. She wasn't certain the chair would remain upright. "What did bring you to Bow Street, if I might ask?"

He chuckled. "An education without expectations or connections." He pushed the chair harder over a little rise. "My choices," he said between rough breaths, "became either fight crime or commit crime."

"You made the proper choice. There is a path that goes to the right just ahead. It winds between those tall grasses."

"I see it. Thank you." He took a breath before resuming their path forward.

"I hear the voices of the others inside the ruin walls," Ann said. "The door is just to the right— *Mr. Martin!*" Ann said on a rising inflection for on the ground, beside the door, lay Mr. Holbein, and this time Ann was sure there was no reviving the man.

Mr. Martin abandoned the wheeled chair and ran to the body. Ann watched him crouch down, then look all around the surroundings. He stood up.

"Lord Ellinbourne! Mr. Nowlton!"

CHAPTER 16

A BODY

Damn Brantley! Ann thought, then looked skyward silently asking for forgiveness. Ladies don't swear, she reminded herself, disgusted at the axiom, but she chafed at being stuck in the chair and placed the blame on Colonel Brantley.

Mr. Holbein was supposed to be locked in that bedchamber. Who had let him out? Even if they weren't suspicious of him, the head injury alone should have kept him confined. She'd seen the white bandage wrapped around his head. She'd also seen the large crimson stain on his white shirt. She watched her uncle and the Duke come out to Mr. Martin and stare down at the body. Then her uncle turned back to the abbey, and she saw him motion others away.

Frustrated, she slapped the arms of the chair. She hated the chair. She hated her ankle and hated being out of what was going on.

Enough being dependent on others!

She pushed herself to stand, holding on to the chairs arms, then she slowly turned around until she could rest her knee on the seat. Hopping, she pushed the chair into a turn so the back faced the abbey.

Yes. This will work!

She pushed herself forward, hopping on one foot while supporting her bad ankle by resting that knee on the chair.

"Whoever did this was not a stranger," she heard Mr. Martin say.

"How do you know that?" the Duke asked.

"The angle of the knife wound is an upward thrust that could only have been done from close in and there is no sign there was a struggle."

"The murderer went that way," Ann said loudly, pointing ahead toward the back corner of the abbey where the tall decorative grasses were crushed.

Three men looked at her. She'd propelled herself to within twenty feet of where they stood.

"Ann!" exclaimed Miles. He ran to her, not aware he'd called her by her first name.

"You shouldn't see this! You shouldn't be here!"

"Well, I am and I did," she said calmly. She turned herself and sat back down in the chair.

"You might as well push me closer," she said.

"No."

She looked at him crossly. "Yes," she countered strongly. She started to stand up again. If he wasn't going to push her in the chair, she would resume her previous way of moving.

"Get her out of here," Nowlton said to Miles.

"Such is my intention." He stopped her by the simple expedient of picking her up.

"What are you doing? Put me down!"

Miles didn't answer her. Instead, he grimly carried her back toward the manor.

"Your Grace!" called out a groom coming out of the stable.

"Saddle a horse," Miles told him. "We need to send for the magistrate."

Ann squirmed in his arms. Carrying her was male posturing. It was embarrassing and ridiculous.

"Stop that," he snapped. "I don't want to drop you. Or would you rather I throw you over my shoulder?"

"You wouldn't," she dared him.

He stopped, looked down at her, "Yes, I would. Part of that Dukely arrogance I've adopted with the title," he told her.

Before she could react, he threw her up and on to his shoulder. He wrapped his arms around the backs of her legs and continued down the path.

Ann gasped at the intimate touch. "No! How dare you!" She pounded his back. "Put me down!" she insisted, loudly. His arms around her legs sent tingling shivers through her. In her heart, she secretly thrilled. This was what the heroes did in her cousin's novels.

He walked around to the front drive just as a carriage drove up. Miles ignored it, his interest solely in getting Ann into the house and in sending for the magistrate.

Ann looked around him at the carriage, mortified at being seen over his shoulder. "Put me down," she hissed. "Do you not see who that is?"

He finally glanced over at the carriage and laughed. The carriage bore the crest of his uncle, the Earl of Galborough.

"What are you laughing for?" Ann asked. "This is embarrassing!"

"You caused this," he said. He walked on.

"I did nothing of the kind. I was useful. I pointed out the bent grasses."

"Which Mr. Martin would have found."

A footman ran out of the house to let down the carriage steps, but slowed when he saw the Duke and Ann, uncertain which he should assist first.

"I told a groom to saddle a horse. When you are finished here, have him fetch the magistrate. There has been a death," Miles said as he climbed the steps before the house.

"Miles!" he heard his uncle call out from the carriage. "What's going on here?"

Miles looked over at his uncle.

"Murder," he called out over his shoulder.

He carried Ann into the house and dumped her unceremoniously on the sofa.

"Really? Really?" she exclaimed. "Was all that theatrics necessary?"

"Yes. Really. Ann—Miss Hallowell, matters have become serious. It was bad enough with Mr. Holbein being hit in the head and then you were shoved and sprained your ankle—"

"Which wouldn't have happened if I didn't have a bad knee," she groused.

"If you hadn't fallen, something else might have occurred. And now we have murder and we do not know why, or by whom. Mr. Holbein seemed an innocent enough young man. Obviously, he wasn't."

There was a flurry of sound from the front hall.

"Miles! Miles Wingate! Ah—there you are!" proclaimed the Earl of Galborough, stomping in through the open parlor door.

Miles straightened and turned toward his uncle. "It is Ellinbourne," he said freezingly, his facial expression a mask.

Ann looked up at him and blinked. This was not a side of the duke she'd seen in the past.

The Earl paused. "Yes, well, old habits and all," he said, his tone more modulated. "But what the bloody hell is going on?"

"Language, your lordship. I shouldn't have to remind you there is a lady present," Miles fairly growled.

The Earl frowned. Ann deduced this was a side of the Duke he hadn't seen before, either. She tried to suppress a grin and failed.

"Pardon, Miss—if you are a Miss," he muttered, "after the way Mi—Ellinbourne carried you in here."

"Enough, Uncle Winsted," Miles said, taking a step toward the man. "This is Miss Hallowell. She has a sprained ankle, not that that should matter, and you are in the house of a Dowager Duchess."

"Galborough," his wife softly admonished from the doorway.

The Earl seemed to deflate. His wife came up beside him and tucked her arm in his. He ran a hand through his hair.

"What did you mean in your letter about Sebastian discovering his lost love or some such nonsense?" the Earl asked more calmly.

"Sebastian met and fell in love with a young woman some months ago."

"Why didn't he introduce her to us?" Lady Galborough asked.

"I believe he would have; however, his butler decided she was not a person you would have approved of and contrived to drive them apart by falsehoods."

Galborough nodded. "Good, then Randolph was acting as we instructed."

"What gave you the right to interfere in his life that way and make that decision?" Ann exclaimed from her seat on the sofa.

Miles walked to the side of the sofa and lightly touched her shoulder.

"Young woman," the Earl began, "my son has a duty to his title and cannot afford to marry willy-nilly. We have a place in society to uphold."

Miles's head jerked up. "And the Quesinberry family is not good enough?"

"Quesinberry!" exclaimed the Earl.

"Yes, as in the Earl of Berry's family. Your son had the good fortune to meet and fall in love with Julia Quesinberry, the niece of the current Earl, who I believe is a crony of yours. Though maybe he won't be any longer when he hears how you considered Miss Quesinberry not good enough."

"Impossible! Randolph told us the woman Sebastian presumed to love is a solicitor's daughter."

Miles crossed his arms over his chest. "Yes, she is. She is the daughter of Hadley Quesinberry."

The Earl stared at him, then slumped down into a nearby chair. "Hadley's daughter? Randolph never gave us names."

"And you gave him fifty pounds for his efforts to drive them apart," Lady Galborough said.

Miles laughed. "I think the butler has profited well."

"Where is Sebastian now?" asked the Earl, tiredly.

"He and the Quesinberrys are on their way to secure a special license. By this time tomorrow, I imagine they will be wed."

"Special license? Why?" asked the Countess.

Miles smiled. "The Duchess deemed it best and sent them on their way."

"But we could have had a splendid wedding!" The Countess frowned at her husband. "Let this be a lesson for you, Winsted Redinger, for our younger offspring. I'm missing my eldest child's wedding," she complained.

"Your Grace," Ann said, looking up at him. As humorous as this exchange with the Galboroughs has been, there were pressing matters. "Would you please ring the bell for the servants? We need to see the Galboroughs to a room for them to rest after their journey and otherwise recover from the surprises today. I also would like my crutches. The Magistrate will be here soon. Frankly, I am surprised the others have not returned to the house."

"Yes, you are quite right. Where are they?" he said as he yanked on the bell pull.

"What's this about a magistrate?" asked the Earl of Galborough.

"There has been a murder," Miles said.

"I heard you say that when we arrived. That was not a joke?"

"I'm afraid not. An associate of Herr Doktor Burkholdt, an art historian from Germany, has been murdered. Ann and the head footman discovered the body as the footman was pushing Miss Hallowell's wheeled chair by the abbey ruin."

"You really can't walk?" asked Lady Galborough.

"I will be able to in a day or so. Last night, I injured my ankle. I need to keep weight off of my foot to let it heal," Ann explained.

"Ha! You admit it!" said Miles.

"What?" Ann said.

"That you need to keep weight off your foot."

"I have not denied that," Ann said. "This is not my first experience with injury."

"Then why did you struggle when I carried you here?" Miles whispered, glancing over at his aunt and uncle. They were quietly arguing.

"Oh, that," she said, a bit sheepishly.

"Yes, that."

Ann was not about to tell him about the heroes in her cousin's novels. That would encourage him too much.

"It was undignified," she said, looking down. In truth, she'd found the experience thrilling. Her body tingled with the memory.

He shook his head. "I'm going to await the magistrate. He should be here soon," Miles said more soberly.

Ann nodded.

He looked at her a moment longer, then left the parlor.

~

MILES KNEW Ann fought the attraction they shared. What he could not understand was why? It was one thing to hold him at bay when she thought Sebastian intended to make her an offer. She was acting honorably there. But now, with Sebastian eloping with his Miss Quesinberry, that reason was gone. Did she truly think he wanted to make her an offer to salvage her pride? The honorable thing to do for his family? He would never do that. Particularly not for his ramshackle cousin.

He knew they were well suited. They enjoyed the arts, conversed easily on a wide range of topics, and shared the same sense of humor. He loved their shared glances and smiles at the foibles of others. He loved being with her. He didn't know when that occurred. They hadn't known each other long, but how long did a person need?

He'd admired her since she read Sebastian's poem.

She adopted none of the feminine dramatics he'd seen in London's marriage mart misses. She was who you saw before you, and he loved that about her, too.

He knew she thought her occasional limp, her trick knee, and the scar on her chin placed her beyond the possibility of a love match and she had convinced herself that the best she could hope for was a marriage of convenience. He thought that a ridiculous belief, but it was her belief. He had to find a way to disabuse her of her notions. They were so not true.

Yes, there was a scar on her chin. However, pox scars were not uncommon in the *ton*. Why should a scar from an accident be considered any differently? And her scar was part of who she was. For when she smiled or laughed, the only thing he—or anyone else —could see was her beautiful face.

And as for her bad knee? She seemed to have managed well with it for several years. He noticed she made use of the handrail when she went up or down the stairs, and she did it unconsciously. Other than last night, it hadn't bothered her and likely wouldn't have if someone hadn't pushed her into the wall.

He headed to the exterior corner of the house to see if he could see Nowlton and Mr. Martin from there.

"*Your Grace! Excuse me, your Grace.*"

Miles turned to see one of the grooms trotting toward him.

"Yes?"

"It's about Colonel Brantley, Your Grace," the man said, coming up to him.

"You're Eddie, correct? I remember Miss Hallowell addressing you when you carried her down the steps in her wheeled chair."

"Yes, Your Grace."

"What is it about Colonel Brantley that you want to tell me."

"He's gone."

"What do you mean he's gone?"

"He asked me to saddle one of Mr. Nowlton's horses. Said he had to urgently get to Malvern Hall."

"Malvern Hall! The home of Lord Candelstone?"

"Yes. Said it was urgent he see Lord Candelstone."

"When did he request the horse?"

"Right after you carried Miss Hallowell into the house."

"Which direction is Malvern Hall and how far away is it?"

"To the northwest. Five miles by road, but just a mite more than three if you cross the fields.

"Your Grace, that is the magistrate's carriage now with Jem riding alongside him."

"Good, I'll lead him to the murder scene. Thank you for telling me about Colonel Brantley. That is curious, but perhaps Nowlton or Lewis may know something."

"Yes, Your Grace," Eddie said, bowing, and turning to walk back to the stables.

Miles returned the way he came to meet the magistrate in the front drive.

"Your Grace!" Jem said as he slid off his horse. "I brought the magistrate as you asked."

"Would you introduce us, please?"

Jem bowed. "Yes, your Grace."

He waited until Eddie came to take the magistrate's carriage.

"Your Grace, this is Sir David Higbee, our magistrate. Sir David, this is the man who had me come get you, the Duke of Ellinbourne."

"I'm pleased to meet you, Your Grace, though one

can always wish meetings were under better circumstances."

"Indeed, sir. I am grateful for you coming so quickly."

"Jem said there has been a murder?"

"Yes," Miles extended his arm to indicate the magistrate should follow him. "A guest of the Duchess, a young man named Jacob Holbein. He was an assistant to another guest, Herr Doktor Burkholdt, an art scholar."

"Who discovered the body?"

"Miss Ann Hallowell, the Duchess's granddaughter, and Lewis, the head footman. Miss Hallowell met with a mishap last night and sprained her ankle. Lewis was pushing her in a wheeled chair toward a side entrance into the monastery. They saw him on the ground near that door."

Miles didn't know why he refrained from mentioning Lewis Martin was a Bow Street agent. Best to let Mr. Martin decide who should know what and when.

Nowlton saw them approach and called out to Mr. Martin, who was at the far corner of the building examining the tall grasses in the area. Mr. Martin carefully picked his way back to Jacob Holbein's body.

"Sir David! Thank you for coming," Nowlton said. "You've met the Duke of Ellinbourne, I see. Let me introduce you to my mother's head footman, Lewis Martin."

Sir David nodded, then looked down at the body in the grass. "A guest, the Duke said."

"Yes. But it is a bit more complicated than him just being a guest," Nowlton said slowly.

"Isn't it always when it comes to murder," the magistrate said drily.

"We have had him locked in a bedroom on the ground floor."

Sir David's head jerked up. "Why?"

"Yesterday he was in a room he hadn't yet been given permission to enter, and while there, someone crashed a large porcelain statue over his head. Dr. Birdsall put seven stitches in the wound."

"Good man, Birdsall," Sir David said.

"Yes. Because there was a possibility Holbein might have been trying to steal the Duchess's Michelangelo sketches that were in there—sketches all the guests seem to covet—we decided to lock him in the bedroom until we could learn more and determine if he actually knew as little as he professed, and was merely a curious viewer of the artwork. And, Dr. Birdsall recommended bed rest for three days," Nowlton explained.

"Someone tried to kill him yesterday and finished the job today," Sir David said. He took a deep breath and let it out slowly.

Miles liked the man. He took his appointed job seriously. He realized he did not know who the magistrate for his area was. Something he would discover on his return.

"I have a bit of information that might be relevant," Miles said.

The three men looked at him. "Colonel Brantley ordered a horse saddled and directions to Malvern Hall."

"Your brother-in-law's estate," said Sir David.

"Yes," said Nowlton.

Lewis looked at Nowlton questioningly, then back at Miles. "When?" he asked.

"Right after I carried Miss Hallowell into the

house. Remember when we interviewed Brantley in the estate room?" Miles asked Nowlton and Lewis.

Nowlton nodded slowly.

"He said: *Someone did not plan their strategy well. Quite surprising.* I thought that an odd thing to say," Miles said. "I tried to ask him how it was surprising, but he brushed it off."

"I remember," Nowlton said.

"I don't know if you are aware, Mr. Martin, but Nowlton's brother-in-law is Lord William Candelstone."

"Formerly of the Home Office. I've read reports on some of his operations," Lewis said.

"Who are you?" Sir David demanded. "You are not a footman."

Lewis bowed. "I beg your pardon, sir. I am a Bow Street agent hired by Mr. Nowlton to investigate certain threats made to the Duchess of Malmsby. The Duchess and Mr. Nowlton thought it best I assume the role of head footman while I am here."

"During the journey here, when Miss Hallowell spoke about her uncle's spying activities, Colonel Brantley became noticeably uncomfortable, so Miss Hallowell changed the topic."

"Mother acquired the Michelangelo sketches during a trip to Sicily arranged by Lord Candelstone," Nowlton mused.

"Miss Hallowell said she, your mother, and Miss Littledean accompanied him and his wife to act as a screen for his activities. He had a network of spies in Italy, and he suspected one of being a traitor. He went to investigate."

"I can't see how any of this can be related to Mr. Holbein, here," Nowlton said.

"The grooms are approaching with a wagon and

stretcher for Mr. Holbein. I suggest we refrain from any more speculation at the moment," suggested Lewis.

The others nodded in agreement.

"I should like to talk to the servants and the guests about who let Mr. Holbein out of the locked bedroom," Sir David said.

"Agreed," said Lewis.

~

"Youse rang, Miss Hallowell," said a under footman almost on the heels of the Duke's departure. Ann didn't recognize him.

"Please inform Mrs. Weaver we have more guests and fetch me my crutches."

The young man trotted out the door, then she heard him break into a run. Ann smiled. Not proper decorum for a footman. She saw Lady Galborough raise one eyebrow at the lad's actions.

Mrs. Weaver was swift to join them in the parlor.

"I saw the carriage draw up," she said. "I've been anticipating the summons."

"Mrs. Weaver, this is the Earl and Countess of Galborough. Please see them settled into rooms. I believe they have had a trying morning and could use a respite."

"Very good, miss."

Mrs. Weaver curtsied and went over to the Galboroughs.

"If your lordship and her ladyship would follow me? I will see you settled and comfortable."

"Mrs. Weaver, on your way, could you please remind that young footman that I still require my crutches?"

Mrs. Weaver bobbed a curtsied. "Yes, miss," she said before leading the Galboroughs to their room.

"Yes, miss?" the young footman said, coming back into the parlor a few minutes later with her crutches. They were almost as long as he was tall.

"Thank you. Go to tell cook to prepare for afternoon tea. I imagine several people might be in need of a fortifying cup of tea."

"Aye, miss," said the young man. "Or a nip," he suggested.

Ann tilted her head. "How long have you been here?" Ann asked. "I don't recall seeing you before."

"I come wit Mr. Martin, miss."

"What's your name?" she asked.

"Dan—er Daniel Wrightson, miss. I been below stairs hepin' Mr. Botsford till Mr. Martin arsked me to come up starrs today on 'count of last night."

"How old are you?"

"Thirteen," he said, throwing out his chest.

She stared at him.

"Almost," he said on a grumble.

"Aren't you a bit young for a footman?"

"I ain't a footman, ax'ually, Miss.

"I didn't think so," Ann said, repressing her smile.

"The ol' Lady—I mean, H'r Grace," he corrected himself, blushing, "she said as how I needed a un'form so that Mrs. Weaver, she gots me this un."

"You look very well in it, too," Ann assured him. "Can you be a footman right now?"

"Yes, miss!"

"Then go tell cook about the tea for this afternoon."

"Yes, miss."

He turned and ran out of the room.

Ann watched him run and laughed to herself.

There was a story there, she was sure. A story for another time, she thought, as she remembered Mr. Holbein.

~

TWENTY MINUTES LATER, the guests began arriving back at the house. Ann laid aside the book she was reading. It had been well over an hour since she and the Duke had left the abbey.

"Oh, my nerves, my shattered nerves! All that blood!" Ann heard Lady Druffner wail.

"We were told to stay away and not look. If you had followed directions, you could have saved your shattered nerves," she heard Lady Oakley retort without an ounce of sympathy.

"You looked," Lady Druffner retorted.

"My nerves don't shatter," Lady Oakley returned as she walked into the gold parlor, Lady Druffner following her.

"Miss Hallowell! You are so lucky not to have been there. Horrible! Horrible! I don't know how long it will take me to recover. Do you have lavender water?" Lady Druffner said on seeing her.

Ann held back a laugh. "I was there, Lady Druffner. I found Mr. Holbein," she said. "Or rather, Mr. Martin—I mean Lewis—and I found him at the same time as Lewis was pushing my chair."

"You were?"

Ann nodded. "I knew immediately he was dead. The Duke was kind enough to bring me back here when he came back to send word for the magistrate," she said, not the least embarrassed about twisting the truth.

Ursula came into the room. "Are you okay, dear?"

she asked. "Mr. Nowlton told us the Duke brought you back here. I've been ever so worried."

"I am fine, and it was a good thing I was here as the Earl and Countess of Galborough arrived as we did."

"Does Vivian know they are here?" Lady Oakley asked.

"I don't believe so, unless Ellinbourne has told her."

Lady Oakley rubbed her hands together. "Oh good. I should love to be the first to tell her and see her reaction."

"Why?" Ann asked, laughing at Lady Oakley's expression.

"Because she is likely plotting again!"

"I don't know. She seemed quite proud with just getting them to leave to get a Special License. She packed them off in her traveling chaise with her coachman."

"Miss Hallowell," said Botsford from the doorway. "Shall I have them bring the tea and refreshments in here?"

"Yes, please, Botsford. And please secure a decanter and glasses from the library for those who might be in need of something stronger."

"Yes, miss, the young lad relayed that need," he said.

He opened the door wider to allow a maid to push in a tea cart. A footman carrying a tray with the glassware for the fortified beverages followed her.

"Would you care for me to pour, miss?" asked the butler.

"Yes, please," said Ann, relieved. Dratted ankle.

Other guests who were still milling about in the hall came into the gold parlor.

Ann hurriedly moved her feet as Lady Oakley

moved to sit next to her. "What did they say?" Lady Oakley whispered.

"Who?"

"Don't be a ninny. The Galboroughs, of course."

"They didn't have an opportunity to say much since the Duke took them to task—though I will say the Earl tried to use the uncle relationship on the Duke to order him around. The Duke wasn't having any of it."

"Bravo for Ellinbourne! And where is he now?"

"The last I knew, he was waiting for the magistrate to arrive."

"That is what Colonel Brantley told me he was going to do," Ursula said, coming over to them with her tea and taking the chair next to the sofa.

"When was that?" Ann asked.

"Right after Mr. Holbein was found, when we were in the abbey."

"The Duke sent a groomsman to get the magistrate. I have not seen Colonel Brantley about. Perhaps he had a horse saddled and rode out to meet the magistrate," Ann suggested.

Ursula frowned. "Perhaps," she said slowly.

"Are you worried about him for some reason?" Ann asked.

Ursula bit her lower lip. "He wasn't in his room last night," she said quietly. She looked about the room. Only Ann and Lady Oakley were near enough to hear her.

"I—"

"Hush," said Lady Oakley. "We understand. You do not need to voice your intentions for last night. Something obviously foiled them for a reason."

Ursula looked like her face would crumple. Ann

reached out and grabbed her hand. "You are very brave," she said.

"Brave?!" How can you say that?" Ursula asked, miserably.

"Brave because you confessed what you knew, even if it might spoil your relationship," Ann said softly.

"I am little better than a strumpet," Ursula said, her facial expression so piteous it almost made Ann laugh.

"Hardly that. Do not berate yourself, and—as the Duke has counseled me—don't make judgements until all the facts are revealed. Strange things have been happening at Versely Park. How much is coincidence and how much is contrivance remains to be sorted out."

CHAPTER 17
DUBIOUS RELATIONS

Though Ann counseled her stepmother to patience, patience eluded Ann. She wanted to talk to Miles. Talking to him helped her get her thoughts straight. She was afraid if she talked to Nowlton or Mr. Martin first, she wouldn't have the opportunity to gather and organize her thoughts.

So, it was Colonel Brantley in the hidden passage, just as she'd thought. Why? And where was he now?

Ann grabbed her crutches and stood up.

Lady Oakley and Ursula, who had been talking quietly, looked up at her. "Do you need me to get you something?" Ursula asked.

"No. I just need to move a bit, even if it is with crutches," she said with a small chuckle.

"Be careful," Lady Oakley said. "With all these people about, someone could easily bump into you, or trip you, and you would be on the floor again."

Ann laughed outright. "True. I will be careful."

She hobbled her way out into the entry hall. While the women seemed to have gravitated to the gold parlor, she judged the man to have gathered in the library by the rise and fall of deep, timbered voices.

John and the boy dressed as a footman, were in the hall.

"Hello, miss, did you need something?" John asked.

"Just trying to move a bit. I get tired of sitting, as you must get tired of standing."

"Yes, miss, that is true."

"Has the magistrate arrived yet?" she asked.

"Yes, miss. He is with His Grace, Mr. Nowlton, and Mr. Martin."

"They'll be bringing the body down soon," Daniel offered from where he stood by the window.

"You are watching out for them?"

"Yes, miss. So we can open the door quickly and bring him in."

"They are bringing him here?"

"Yes, on 'ccount it would upset the horses ta take him to the stable," Daniel said with an air of superior knowledge.

"Well, I guess I'm glad someone is seeing to the horses' sensibilities," Ann said, fighting back a laugh.

"Beg pardon, miss," John said while shaking his head at Daniel's explanation. "They are bringing him in so Mrs. Weaver can clean and dress his body," John explained. "It will only be for a couple of hours before Mr. Johnson finishes making a coffin."

"I guess I hadn't thought about what needs to be done for a murdered man, particularly one who has been a houseguest," she said. "Do you know if anyone has gone into his room to look for papers that might tell us of his family?"

"No, miss, I don't."

"They're coming this way!" Daniel cried out.

"Miss, you had best rejoin the ladies in the parlor while they bring the body in."

"I'm sure I won't faint, but I know my uncle would take exception to my presence. Tell Nowlton, His Grace, and Mr. Martin I want to speak with them, as I have information they need to hear."

"Yes, miss," John said with a bow.

AN HOUR LATER, Miles excused himself from the murder investigation conversations and went in search of Ann. He discovered her sitting on the back terrace which overlooked the cutting gardens which the Duchess used to such advantage.

"Here you are! I have been looking for you," he said as he closed the glass paned terrace door behind him.

She turned her head up to look at him and smiled. "I came out here for some quiet," she said.

"And here I come to disturb your peace."

"No! No! Not at all. Please, sit down," she invited, indicating the chair beside her. "I would have preferred to sketch than to just sit here. The flowers are so beautiful this spring; however, it is difficult to carry my supplies and use my crutches. Bothersome things."

"We should get you a leather satchel, such as I use," he said as he sat down. He stretched his legs out. He'd been standing in conversation for considerably more than an hour.'

"We?" she asked archly.

"I," he corrected. "My present to you."

"Thank you. But you don't have to do that."

"I would like to," he said, looking at her intently.

Ann felt the heat of a blush stain her checks. She looked down at her hands clasped in her lap.

She cleared her throat. "That is most kind of you,

Your Grace," she managed to get out past the sudden lump in her throat.

He wasn't the most handsome man she'd ever met. But there was a warm sureness and calmness about him she found particularly appealing.

She'd been thinking about him a great deal as she sat out here, her eyes occasionally tearing up as she considered their positions in life. If only he hadn't inherited the Ellinbourne title!

She studied his profile as he looked out across the gardens. A warm tingling stirred within her. She realized she'd taken it for granted that a marriage with Miles could not happen. Why was she certain she could not marry him? Would that be true for any duke, or only this duke? Where did these thoughts come from? She was suddenly seeing him with new eyes.

He turned toward her. "It is very peaceful and beautiful out here. You were right to seek peace here."

He uncrossed his legs and leaned forward, his forearms resting on his knees. "John said you had something to tell us. Do you need all of us here, or do you want to tell me first?"

"It probably doesn't matter. It's about Colonel Brantley."

"Yes?"

"He wasn't in his room last night."

"How do you know that?"

She smiled. "To say would be to betray a lady's trust."

"I understand completely." His expression sobered, then he frowned. "Colonel Brantley left shortly after you and Mr. Martin discovered Jacob Holbein's body."

"Never say so!"

He straightened as he nodded. "Requested a horse be saddled. As the groom prepared the horse, Colonel Brantley asked him how far it was to Malvern Hall and what was the best way to get there from here."

"Malvern Hall! But that is Uncle William and Aunt Catherine's estate!"

He breathed in deeply. "Yes. It has us wondering if this matter could be related to his days with the Home Office and if so, how? It doesn't make any sense."

Ann thought back to her days in Sicily where they acquired the sketches.

"I remember the last day Lady Blessingame was with us at Villa di Fiori." She looked off across the gardens—only seeing memories instead.

"BRR-R-R, but it's cold and drafty up here!" Helena exclaimed, the heavy door banging against the wall with her brisk, forthright entrance. Her black paisley shawl fell off one shoulder and dragged along the floor behind her.

"No colder than yesterday morning, cuz," rejoined Ann, laughter coloring her voice as she followed her energetic cousin into the upper-story room, formerly the schoolroom, now given over to the cataloguing and crating of the fabulous painting collection of Lady Travis, a crony of the Dowager Duchess of Malmsby.

"Well, I should be only too glad when this task is done. This space reminds me more of a dungeon than a schoolroom," Helena said, scanning the dark room with its tiny square windows set high on the walls.

Lady Isabella Blessingame, crouching near a stack of framed artwork at the end of the room, stood up and shook the dust from her black skirts. "Little difference to its earlier

inhabitants, I should think," she said with brittle bright-
ness. She stepped out of the shadows and into the circle of
light cast by the lantern set on the long table that stood in
the center of room.

Ann noted the fine tremble in their friend's hand as
Bella flipped open the ledger book into which they'd been
cataloguing the paintings, prints, sketches, and statues.
"I've been feeling quite low that I should be leaving you
with so much yet to do, but in reviewing the ledger, I am
surprised to find we are nearly done."

Her voice rang off the stone walls with forced bright-
ness. Helena and Ann exchanged concerned glances.

"I was just saying the same to Helena before we came
up," Ann said, laying a hand on Bella's arm. "And we do
sincerely thank you for your help."

Helena nodded.

Ann looked carefully at Lady Isabella. "Are you feeling
quite all right?"

"What?" Isabella turned her startled glance in Ann's
direction, then looked away. "Oh-- Yes. Just a little
headache." She looked down at the ledger again.

"You can't wish to embark on a carriage journey down
the coast with an aching head," Ann said. "Why don't you
go to your chamber and lie down."

Isabella glanced back at the stacks of paintings. "Yes,
perhaps I will," she said, her voice sighing out.

"WHEN I THINK about that day, I am struck with how
nervous Lady Isabella seemed. At the time, I took it as
part of her bereavement, but now I wonder. I remember her crouching down in front of a stack of
paintings we had already catalogued. It didn't occur to
me to ask what she was doing. And when she turned

the page of our ledger book, her hand trembled slightly. She said she had a headache. Now I wonder."

"How did she get along with Lord Candelstone?" Miles asked.

"She didn't." Ann cocked her head to the side. "She tried to stay away from him, to not be in the same room with him. She always had to be somewhere else. But she couldn't hide at meals. I think if she could have, she would have taken all her meals in her room. Uncle insisted she join us. There were a couple times she met with Uncle William privately, meetings she couldn't get out of and afterward it would take a good hour or so for her to regain her disposition. Though she was in mourning, for the most part she was pleasant company--except around Uncle William."

"Why was that?" Miles asked.

"She blamed Uncle William for her husband's death," Ann said. "I don't know the details; however, I gather Lord Blessingame would not have been where he was and killed if he hadn't been ordered there by Lord Candelstone. She believed my uncle unnecessarily put him at risk."

"Interesting."

"But that was over two years ago."

"I know. Is that the only time Candelstone has had anything to do with the Duchess's art collection?"

"As far as I know, yes."

Miles rose and extended his hand to Ann. "I think we need to talk to Nowlton and Mr. Martin." He drew her to her feet and handed her crutches to her. "How is the ankle?" he asked and she positioned the crutches in place.

"Sore, but better. I have to counsel myself to not walk on that foot."

"Best if you don't. And if the crutches become too uncomfortable, I—"

"No, I do not want that wheeled chair!" Ann said emphatically.

"I was going to say I could always carry you."

Ann blushed, and her body suddenly tingled. "That won't be necessary," she said quickly.

"Coward," the Duke said softly.

"You are teasing me!"

"Yes, do you mind so?"

"No, actually I don't!" she admitted. She dipped her head down a bit. "I rather like it," she said softly.

Miles laughed. "Me, too." He walked ahead to open the terrace door for her.

The gold parlor was empty except for Lady Druffner and Mrs. Morrison working on their respective needlework. Mrs. Morrison looked up.

"If you are looking for the Duchess, she and the other guests are in the library, taking turns answering Sir David's questions," she said.

"Didn't he want to ask you any questions?"

"Yes, but I have no interest in hearing what others have to say. When he needs me, he will call for me."

"Lady Druffner, is that your attitude as well?"

"Attitude? I don't believe I have an attitude. No, no. It is too crowded in there."

"I imagine it is," said Miles. He turned to Ann. "It might be best if you did take to the wheeled chair," he said. "Maneuvering with crutches in a crowded room is inviting another accident."

Ann screwed up her lips in a sneer. Miles laughed.

"Perhaps no one has brought it back to the house yet," she suggested.

"Let's find out." He pushed a chair out of her direct path and opened the parlor doors. John was out in the hall. "John, did Miss Hallowell's chair get returned to the house?"

"I brought it back," Daniel piped up. "It is over here, in this little room." Daniel ran to get it.

"I haven't seen him before," Miles observed.

"I just met him today. His name is Daniel. He came with Mr. Martin."

"His son?"

"I don't believe so."

"Here you are, miss!" Daniel said, running out of the anteroom, pushing the chair. The chair careened forward as Daniel slid to a halt on the marble floor. Miles grabbed the chair before its momentum carried it into Ann.

"Thank you!" Ann said breathlessly. "I had a sudden vision of landing on the floor again, done in by a wheeled chair."

"Sit," Miles said. "Daniel will take charge of your crutches."

"Yes, miss," the boy said, taking them from her. He tried to put them under his arms as Ann did; however, they were too tall. He made a face, then carried them away.

When they came into the library, Sir Robert was telling the magistrate how he was studying the porcelain ware when Mr. Holbein was hit over the head. No one could have missed seeing him there.

"That is true," Miles whispered, leaning over the chair to speak to Ann. "A rotund figure dressed all in black, looking like a black French Crèvecœur chicken.

She playfully pushed him away as she tried to suppress laughter.

"And where did you go when you left the dining room following nuncheon?"

"I went upstairs to my room. I wanted to change

my cravat as I'd somehow managed to get a spot of grease on the one I was wearing."

"Did anyone see you go upstairs?"

"I have no idea. Possibly," he shrugged.

"I saw him head up the stairs," Lady Peverley offered.

"Did you see him come back down?"

"No."

"Why all these questions of us," demanded Lord Druffner. "Look about you. There is one person missing. I'd bet a pony he's the one you need to talk to."

"Lord Druffner, I will question Colonel Brantley in due time. We believe we know where he went. Right now, I am establishing where everyone was and who they were with." Sir David patiently explained. "All bits of information that can be collected should be collected as soon as possible else memories fade or become embroidered. It is tedious, but necessary."

"Humph."

The Marquis of Peverley crossed his legs and leaned back in his chair. He raised his head, looking down his nose at Lord Druffner. "If I can suffer through this, you can as well," he drawled.

"Sir Robert, how long were you upstairs?"

Sir Robert entwined his fingers on his ample stomach as he considered the question. "About twenty minutes. When I came down, I went into the library."

"Was anyone else in there?"

"Lord Wolfred and Herr Doktor Burkholdt. We stayed there until a footman came to tell us the party was gathering to go to the abbey."

"Thank you, Sir Robert. Now—"

The front door banged open. The sudden noise stopping Sir David from finishing. They all looked toward the door. Loud voices came from the hall.

"I know my way."

"That's my Uncle!" Ann whispered to Miles right before the library door opened.

Lord William Candelstone strode into the room, Colonel Brantley following behind.

"Vivian Nowlton, this is all your fault. Why couldn't you just sell the damned sketches? I assure you, none of this would have happened if you had."

"And what would you know of it, Silly Billy?" she asked, calling him by his long-ago childhood nickname to remind him she was his elder. She sat in a winged chair by the fireplace, frowning at Candelstone.

Lord Candelstone flushed. "I need those sketches," he ground out.

"You are not an art enthusiast," the duchess said flatly. "And if you need them so badly, why not ask me for them?"

"I was trying to keep the knowledge I had regarding the sketches private."

"So, you are the person offering 1000 pounds over the Duchess's sale price for the sketches," Nowlton declared. "Do you realize she has had threats because of this?"

Candelstone ran his hand over his balding head. "That was not supposed to happen."

"And that is what you meant, isn't it Colonel Brantley, when you said it wasn't a well thought out strategy? You knew it was Lord Candelstone who wanted the sketches," said Miles.

Colonel Brantley reluctantly nodded. "I was to quietly put who ever bought the sketches in contact with Lord Candelstone."

"You've been using me!" Ursula cried out, rising from her seat on the sofa.

"Now, Mrs. Hallowell, Ursula—" Colonel Brantley said soothingly as he approached her.

Ursula ran behind the sofa and around it, tears streaming down her cheeks. She escaped out of the room before he could follow her.

"This was badly done, William, very badly done," said Lady Peverley. "I am so glad I quit working for you over a year ago."

Ann and Miles looked at each other. The Marchioness of Peverley once spied for Candelstone?

The Marquis rose from his chair and came over to his wife. He laid a reassuring hand on her shoulder. She covered his hand with her own.

Ann was beginning to understand what was going on. This was about her uncle's spy network. "This has to do with our trip to Sicily two years ago, doesn't it?" she said.

Candelstone looked at her in surprise, but did not disagree.

"Was something hidden in those framed sketches?"

Her uncle stared at her in silence.

"Mr. Martin," said the Duchess, turning to look at him standing behind her, leaning against the fireplace. "Would you be so kind as to fetch the Michelangelo sketches?"

"Certainly, Your Grace," Lewis said, straightening.

Lord Candelstone glared at him. "Who are you?"

"Lewis Martin of Bow Street," Lewis said as he walked toward the door.

"Bow Street!" exploded Lord Druffner.

Those in the room began to talk loudly, all asking what a Bow Street agent was doing at the Duchess's house party.

"I hired Mr. Martin because of those threats my

mother received," said Nowlton. He looked at his brother-in-law. "Does Catherine know what you have been about?"

"I doubt it," his mother drily said from her chair.

"Leave Catherine out of this," Candelstone said.

"Hard to do that now, this is a family affair," said Nowlton. One side of his lips curled up. "I almost pity you."

Candelstone's face took on a mottled, angry hue. "This does not concern her."

"Then you are a fool if you think so."

Ann's attention was caught by a movement to the side of the room. It was Herr Doktor Burkholdt and his wife. Their heads were bent down, and they were talking in whispers with each other. By their posture, Ann rather thought they were attempting to not be noticed. She tapped Miles's hand.

"Look at the Burkholdts," she whispered.

Miles looked over at them at the same time Burkholdt looked up and saw his regard. Burkholdt ducked his head down again.

"Strange," he said to Ann.

"I agree."

Lewis returned with the sketches. He walked over to the desk to lay them down.

The Duchess rose from her chair and crossed to the desk. She opened a side drawer and drew out her jeweled handle, sharp, slim paper knife she used for cutting apart pages of new books. She laid it on the table.

"As carefully as possible, please," she said to him.

"Of a certainty, Your Grace," he solemnly replied. He picked up one of the frames.

"Wait!" yelled Lord Candelstone. He shifted to the

right to see the back corner of the room. "I know you!" he cried, pointing at the Burkholdts.

The Duchess frowned at her son-in-law. "That's Doktor Burkholdt and his wife."

"No," Candelstone countered, "that's Hans Gruemann and Lily Gruemann, the nemesis of the Home Office, spies who worked for whoever paid the most," he explained as he stepped toward them.

"But—" the Duchess cried out, turning to look at them.

Lily Gruemann leaped from her seat on the sofa, lunged forward to grab the paper knife off the desk, then grabbed the Duchess and held the blade to her throat.

Ann screamed. The men rose to their feet. Lily pressed the knife edge closer to the Duchess's throat. "Don't move. Anyone!" She looked about the room, her eyes narrowed.

"Ve vill leave now," she said. "Hans, ze sketches, get sem!" she ordered as she pulled the Duchess against her, and sidestepped to the door.

Hans Gruemann scuttled forward and picked up the framed sketches. He held them tightly against his chest with one arm, his eyes darting about the room. With his other hand, he pulled a handkerchief out of his pocket and mopped his brow.

"Do not try vhat you are thinking, Mr. Bow Street agent, or anyone else," Lily Gruemann warned. 'Zis knife, it is sharp, and pressed against her neck. I could kill her vaster zan you could reach me." She laughed harshly. "And I have no problem vith ze killing, as I killed zat fool Jacob Holbein who vould double cross us."

Burkholdt nodded agreement. "Zat one, she has

no soul," he said as he worked his way toward the door from the other side of the desk.

Lily edged her way toward Ann and Miles. With Ann's wheeled chair pushed into the room, her path was narrow. She glanced to her side to avoid furniture as she pulled the Duchess with her.

Ann watched Lily. Around her, she was aware of others in the room, visibly tense, looking for an opportunity to intervene. She would be the closest. What could she do, she wondered, stuck as she was in a wheeled chair?

No, not stuck.

The idea came fast. She would have one chance.

Lily glanced aside again. Ann surged up out of the chair, catching Lily's arm and pushing it up and away from her grandmother's neck. Her momentum carried her against Lily and her grandmother. The three women crashed to the floor, the wheeled chair falling over on them. Ann felt it hit and pain shoot through her bad ankle, but she held on to Lily's arm. The woman screamed. She yanked the Duchess's hair, bucked and kicked at them to get them off her.

Ann fought the woman for the knife, pushing her knife arm to the floor.

Miles stomped on Lily's hand. She dropped the knife as she yowled in pain. The Duchess rolled off Lily's arm. Lewis swiftly grabbed Lily's arm and twisted it around her back. Miles grabbed her other arm, kicking the knife out of the way.

Ann took a couple of deep breaths. It was over. She trembled, her eyes watering. She pushed ineffectually at the chair.

Lord Peverley came forward to right the wheeled chair and pulled it away. Lady Peverley put her arms under Ann to help her up. "You did good," she whispered to her.

From outside the library came a loud crack, followed by a crash and a howl of pain.

"Burkholdt!" Colonel Brantley yelled. He ran out of the library, followed by Lord Candelstone.

"I didn't mean to break it!" exclaimed a young voice.

CHAPTER 18

REVELATIONS

Colonel Brantley and John, the footman, escorted a limping Hans Gruemann into the library. Behind them came Lord Candelstone with the sketches, their frames cracked and splintered. Behind him followed young Daniel dragging a broken crutch. He brought it over to Ann.

"I'm rite sorry, Miss, I dinna means to break it," he said, handing the broken, useless crutch to her.

"How did this happen?" she asked him gently.

"I were playing with it," he admitted sheepishly. "I swung it around to plant on the floor, then I'd go flying. It were great!" he explained, his eyes shining, then he sobered. "That man came outta the library whilst I were swinging it," he said, pointing at Mr. Gruemann, "and it caughts him behind his knees." He pointed to a spot behind his own knee. "He fell, the crutch fell, the pictures fell---everything fell," he said, throwing up his hands, "and broked the crutch. I'm sorry," he said again.

She looked at the crutch he'd handed to her. "I'm sure Mr. Johnson can either repair this one or make me a new one. Do not worry. You are actually a hero, you know."

"Me?"

"You made it possible for Colonel Brantley and John to capture this man."

"Oh!"

"Daniel," said Lewis, "Do you know where some rope is?"

"Yes!" he said, his exuberance returning.

"Fetch it, please, so we can tie these two up."

"Yes, sir." He went running out of the room.

"Let's see what so special about these sketches, now," said Sir Robert, rubbing his hands together.

"Not until we get the Gruemanns tied up. Our curiosity might take our attention away from these two, giving them an opportunity to escape. I don't want to chance that."

"Yes, yes. Of course," Sir Robert said despondently.

"Are you all right, Grandmother?" Ann asked as she saw her grandmother limping across the room to the bell pull, her hair in wild disarray, the flounce of her dress torn and dragging behind her.

"Yes, I'm just not as young as I once was. Might have to ask Mr. Johnson to make two sets of crutches."

"Probably best if you have this chair," Ann replied.

"No, thank you. I've sat in that chair before, and it is as uncomfortable as you found it to be."

"Then why insist I sit in it?"

"I thought it might feel different for you."

Ann rolled her eyes.

"Yes, Your Grace?" said Botsford from the library door. His eyes widened slightly at the Duchess's appearance but didn't say anything. He glanced about the room with interest.

"Raid the cellar. We'll want the best port and brandy you can find."

"Right away, Your Grace."

Daniel ducked underneath Botsford's arm, running into the room with his discovered rope.

Sir David took the rope from Daniel. He measured out a length to use for tying the two up, picked up the paper knife from the floor, and cut the rope. "I'm afraid cutting the rope will dull your paper knife," Sir David said as he handed a length of the rope to Lewis.

The Duchess shrugged. "I don't know if I would wish to use that paper knife again, anyway. It would be a constant reminder."

He nodded as he cut off a second piece of rope and handed it to Colonel Brantley.

"Can we secure them somewhere until I am ready to take them?" Sir David asked.

"There is a small anteroom off the entrance hall. We can lock them in there and my footman here can guard the room so there are no more escapes," the Duchess said, gesturing at John.

"Excellent. Mr. Martin, Colonel Brantley?" Sir David said, gesturing them to go ahead of him with their prisoners.

When they returned, Mr. Botsford was filling brandy glasses.

When everyone had their glass, they toasted the Duchess's health, then the Duchess motioned to Lewis to dismantle the broken frames.

"No need to do that, I'll take those," said Lord Candelstone.

"Mr. Martin, if he so much as touches those, arrest him for theft," declared the Duchess.

"Gracious!" Ann whispered.

Miles squeezed her shoulder in agreement.

"Your Grace!" objected Candelstone.

"Hush and sit. You will have your chance to explain this mess. Mr. Martin, please continue."

Lewis carefully cut away the glued paper backing from the frame of the first sketch, then carefully lifted the sketch out. He laid it on the desk.

"One moment, please," said Lord Peverley. He got up and crossed to a bookshelf with tall books. He selected one and brought it over to the desk. "Let's put the sketches between the leaves of this book to protect them out of their frames."

Lewis picked up the sketch again. Lord Peverley opened the book and Lewis slid the picture in.

Lewis went back to examining the frame. He looked all along the frame, inside and out, but didn't not find any place where there could be a hidden message. He pushed the frame aside and drew the second frame toward him. Again, he carefully cut away the paper. Halfway around, he stopped.

"There is already a very thin slit cut in this paper." After showing everyone the frame, he cut the paper backing away.

There was a folded sheet of paper behind the sketch. He carefully unfolded it.

"No!" protested Lord Candelstone.

Lewis scanned the paper and looked up. "I don't think this is the paper you are expecting. It's a letter," he said. He handed it to the Duchess.

She shook her head. "My eyes are not as good as they used to be, and I don't have my glasses. —Ann, would you read this, please?"

Lewis passed the paper to Ann.

Ann looked at the date. It was the day Lady

Blessingame left Villa de Fiori. She glanced at the signature.

Miles looked at it from over her shoulder.

"It's from Lady Blessingame," she said. She read aloud:

April 12, 1814

Villa de Fiori, Sicily

Dear Lord Candelstone,

I disagreed with you about the lists, but you wouldn't listen to my reasoning. You don't listen to anyone but yourself.

We learned today Napoleon has been defeated and has abdicated.

Hoorah for us all! The people on your list, the spies on our side and the spies on Napoleon's side need a respite. The war has gone on too long.

When my husband acquired this list for you it cost him his life. This list, in the wrong hands, could cost more lives, even with Napoleon's abdication. Enough. I am tired, I am a widow after less than a year of marriage.

I told you I hid the list in one of the Michelangelo sketches going to your mother-in-law, that you could retrieve it later, if you needed it. I said it was best if neither of us had it in our possession, for that potential cost of lives reason I gave you.

I lied. I didn't hide it. I burned it.

My kind regards to your wife, Catherine. She is a wonderful woman.

Sincerely,

Isabella

Lady Harry Blessingame

Ann softly finished reading. She laid the letter in her lap.

"How dare she," demanded Lord Candelstone, his

face mottled with rising anger. "That list was government property. I should have her arrested for destroying vital government papers."

"If they were so vital, why has it taken you two years to even try to recover them?" snapped the Duchess.

"Because I'm talking to some people about—" he stopped suddenly, gritting his teeth.

"About starting a private network," stated Lady Peverley. "That's what you were fishing about in letters to me," she said.

"A private spy network? One not directly reporting to the government?" Miles asked, incredulous.

"They haven't done anything right since I retired. Bloody Hell, we have insurgents in our country trying to upset our government and the English way of life. We need to ferret these traitors out and destroy them before they become too powerful. I've been having conversations with like-minded gentlemen in government. We are investigating the opportunity to create a new force. That list of our spies could have proven useful for recruitment purpose. Now it is gone. Stupid woman."

"That is enough!" said the Duchess. "Isabella was in mourning, and you never once acknowledged her feelings the entire time she was with us in Sicily. Not once did you give her an ounce of sympathy, never tried to console her for her grief. You just bullied her."

"She needed to follow orders," Candelstone returned.

"Why? Was she in your employ?" the Duchess asked.

Ann saw Lady Peverley shake her head *No*.

"No, but her husband was," Candelstone ground out.

"And because her husband was, that gives you the right to order her around as well?"

"Well—" he paused. "That's not—" He compressed his lips.

"You made a mistake, Silly Billy," the Duchess said softly, using the childhood moniker. "A mistake in how you treated Lady Blessingame, a mistake in thinking to start another spy network, and a mistake in doing whatever it was you did that got you pressured into retirement. Makes me wonder how many other mistakes you've made. I pity my daughter married to you. Then again, I wonder how your life will proceed when Catherine discovers your machinations."

"Excuse me, you Grace," Sir David said into the growing silence after the Duchess delivered her dressing down. "I should need a wagon to convey the Gruemanns to jail and the assistance of Lord Candelstone and Colonel Brantley, as they have prior knowledge of the couple, and the help of Mr. Martin, as well, if I might."

The Duchess inclined her head. "Capital idea, Sir David. The sooner the Burkholdt, or Gruemanns, or whatever their names, are gone, the better. Mr. Martin, would you see to a wagon?" She turned back to Candelstone as Lewis left the library.

"Silly Billy, you may leave. And take Colonel Brantley, your sycophant, with you." The Duchess commanded. She looked at Colonel Brantley. "I will have your luggage and your valet sent to Malvern Hall." She waved her hand dismissively at them, and despite the mussed hair and torn gown, Ann didn't think she'd ever seen her grandmother look so elegant and powerful.

Ann turned her head to look at Miles. He nodded. She smiled and looked back at her grandmother.

Lord Peverley was by the desk, looking at the second sketch. Carefully, he picked it up and put it between two other pages in the big book he'd brought over. He quietly returned to his seat next to his wife. She reached over to take his hand in hers.

The Duchess nodded her approval of what he'd done.

"My lord," she said. "You truly have an appreciation for sketches and prints. I am awed, for so many feign a love of art, but yours goes beyond love. You also know it and display a deep respect for it."

"Thank you, Your Grace," he said, inclining his head.

"For that reason, I would like to offer to sell the Michelangelo sketches to you."

"No!" said Sir Robert. "You can't."

"You haven't heard my offer yet!" cried out Lord Wolfred.

The Duchess held up her hand to stop their importuning.

"Well, my lord?" she said to Peverley

"How much do you want for them?" he asked.

The Duchess leaned back in her chair and took a deep breath. "I want a guinea for each deposited in the poor box of my village church."

"I accept," the Marquis said with alacrity.

"No!" cried out Sir Robert, jumping out of his seat.

"And—" the Duchess continued to Lord Peverley, "I want you to preserve them as you have instructed us and promise not to resell them for a period of five years."

Peverley looked at his wife and squeezed her hand. He looked back at the Duchess. "Lady Peverley and I will be delighted to fulfill your wishes."

"Good. Now that that is settled, I suggest we retire

to our rooms to dress for dinner. I know there is more to discover; however, the sooner I can put this day's activities behind me, the better I shall feel," she said as she rose from her chair. She walked with her head erect, her back straight, and a pronounced limp as she led them out of the room.

CHAPTER 19
MEETING OF THE MINDS

The next morning Miles found Ann on the terrace, petting a black and white cat who'd curled up in her lap.

"Who's your friend? I haven't seen him before," he asked, sitting down in the chair next to her wheeled chair.

"This is Mr. Peabody," Ann replied, smiling down at the cat. "He doesn't like people much, doesn't like crowds, rather like me." A thoughtful expression spread across her face.

"No-o-o," she said slowly, "that is not quite true. I enjoy being with other people, but afterwards I need time away. That's why Ursula went to so many more social activities than I did. I wanted time to myself. When the invitations came to the house, we would go through them together and select the ones to attend and which ones to send regrets. I sent more regrets than acceptances," she said, smiling in memory as she scratched behind the cat's ears.

He purred.

"I'm not overly fond of social events, either," Miles said. "Though my reasons are different." He reached over to give the cat a scratch. The feline stretched. "Besides the late hours and aggravation with the gossip and posturing that goes on at those events, they get in the way of my creativity. I do my best work in the morning."

"So, you have solved that problem by not going to London," Ann said with a smile.

Mr. Peabody jumped off her lap and sauntered toward the terrace stone steps.

He shrugged. "I'm primarily a landscape painter. I enjoy painting a vista during different times of the day, under different weather conditions. I am fascinated by light and shadow and the varying colors that appear."

"Which is why you are fascinated with the abbey," she said.

He looked in the direction of the abbey, hidden around the corner of the house. "Yes. The other evening the colors glowing on the stones were astonishing." Recalling that scene, his face transfused with wonder and delight.

She reached across the space between them to lay her hand on his arm. He laid his other hand on hers. "Then stay here a week or two more," she said impulsively. "To paint, I mean. I should be glad of the company," she added, suddenly shy, pulling her hand away. "I will not return to London until my ankle is better, and under the circumstances, Ursula is not keen to return right away."

He looked at her intently. "I have to return to London before the Royal Academy of Art's new exhibit opens."

"Yes! I should like to see the exhibit, too. When it opens, that is."

Ann didn't know why she suddenly felt as flustered as a schoolgirl, but she did.

"Ann, is it too soon to ask?" Miles whispered.

Ann looked up at him. "Not if you really mean it, and this is not pity for your cousin's actions," she said.

"Pity! I could not marry anyone because of the ill-conceived actions of another. You enchanted me from the moment I saw you at your townhouse. I thought you were your stepmother, and it crushed me to discover you were my cousin's intended. Emotions flooded me in a way I'd never experienced before. It was confusing. I don't know if that is what they call love at first sight; however, it was certainly fascination at first sight," he said.

"That unexpected flood of emotion greatly colored my reactions to Redinger's treatment of you. I was so angry with that poem he had me deliver. I stormed back into his townhouse, grabbed him by his banyan collar, and shook him. If his friends hadn't been in the room, I don't know what I would have done.

"No, I mean every word I am going to say to you." He turned in his chair and took her hands in his. "Ann Hallowell, will you be my wife? Will you be my Duchess?"

"Yes and yes! And if I could, if I wasn't recovering from a second injury to my ankle, I would throw myself into your arms."

"And shower me with kisses?" he asked playfully.

"And shower you with kisses," Ann affirmed, laughing.

"I think I should like that," he said. "I shall have to stay a few more weeks here then with my fiancé. Maybe even get some of those kisses when there aren't so many people about," he said, looking through the terrace doors to the gold parlor where some guests mingled.

"A masterful plan," said Ann.

"Shall we go in and tell your grandmother to send for Mr. Quesinberry?" he asked, assuming a sober mien.

"I believe we should," Ann said, trying to be equally sober, and failing. She could not stop smiling.

EPILOGUE
FAMILY TIES

"How is it coming?" Ann asked Miles as she walked into the Versely Park library with the aid of a cane two weeks later.

"I've just finished."

"Good. I can scarcely believe all that has happened in the ten days since we left London, and we return to the city tomorrow, an affianced couple," she said with a delighted smile as she sat down at the desk opposite him.

"To prepare for our next adventure," suggested Miles.

"Yes!" she enthused. "And speaking of a next adventure, have you read Sir David's report on our completed adventure? He certainly is a thorough gentleman."

"He is what a magistrate should be."

Ann agreed. "In the report it says there really is a Herr Doktor Burkholdt who was intending to come here. He received a missive of a family illness that demanded he return to Germany immediately. He requested his assistant, Jacob Holbein to send his regrets to the Duchess, but he didn't."

"He really was Burkholdt's assistant?"

"Yes. He and Burkholdt had heard about the thousand pound offer for the sketches and discussed that. Herr Doktor wanted to take the sketches back to Germany but was tempted by the money offer, if he could get the Duchess to part with the sketches. Holbein contacted the Gruemanns, who he knew through the embassy, and together they decided to try to get the sketches for themselves. Holbein coached Gruemann on Art History and art history terms so he could fake his knowledge."

"They went to a great deal of effort for a thousand pounds."

"The money was an added benefit. Gruemann wanted that list. Remember how my uncle said he played for whoever paid him the most money? At one time he helped England and learned about the list then—helped create it, actually. And he knew the rumor that the list was in an artwork in the possession of the Duchess of Malmsby."

Miles nodded. "When the opportunity fell into his lap to retrieve the list and make some money on the side, he went for it."

"At the urging of Frau Gruemann."

"Did they send the threatening letters to the Duchess?"

"No! Would you believe Lord Wolfred did that!"

"Wolfred was that desperate for them?"

"Something about debts."

Miles shook his head. "Sad.--Who hit Holbein on the head?"

"Frau Gruemann, who also picked Donna's apron pocket for the bedroom key after Donna took Holbein food, she then unlocked the door, and convinced the young man they had to get away."

"Why did she go to all that effort to kill the man?"

"She didn't want to share the money."

Miles gave a snort of laughter. "Defeated by greed. If she hadn't wanted to get rid of Holbein they might have pulled this off—except for getting the list they wanted."

"Grandmother was quite taken with the idea of an art history professor. We have nothing like that in England. She didn't question him deeply. He fooled everyone."

"What about that conversation you heard outside the library?"

"That was Brantley and Peverley. They were trying to learn about the list in case it had already been found."

"A reasonable thought that it might, given the slit in the back of the frame backing."

"Yes, and why they were searching the house," she said. "That's also why Brantley was in the passage, which he knew about from my uncle. Uncle told him —explicitly--to search there, why, I can't imagine," she said, shaking her head.

"Brantley wanted the list for my uncle. Peverley wanted the list in order to destroy it because he knew his wife's name was on it," she explained. "I also learned that Brantley met Ursula at my uncle's London townhouse. It was an arranged introduction, so yes, he was charged with instructions from my uncle to ingratiate himself with her. But, according to Brantley, he has fallen in love with her and is now despondent because of the way they met. I don't know if I believe him or not. It is for them to sort out."

"Precisely. Just as we now need to sort out our lives," Miles said. "Would you like to read what I wrote to Adam?"

"Yes."

"Here it is."

Ann came around the desk to read over Miles's shoulder, resting her hands on his shoulders as she leaned forward.

Miles was enchanted by the slight scent of lavender that wafted from her. He couldn't wait to make this woman his.

APRIL 30, 1816

  Versely Park

  Dear Adam,

  If the family gossip lines of communication are working at speed, you have no doubt heard that our cousin, Sebastian Redinger, has been married by special license to Miss Julia Quesinberry, Lord Berry's niece. Why special license? Not for any ruinous reasons. But, that is a tale best told over a pint of ale.

  I wouldn't mind a marriage by special license either, for I have found my Duchess and am eager to claim her. However, as the aunts and my mother would be horrified if I did a special license nuptial, the banns will be posted this Sunday.

  Her name is Ann Hallowell, the daughter of the late Mr. and Mrs. Graham and Maria Hallowell, grand-daughter of the Dowager Duchess of Malmsby.

  Why this woman before all others? There are a dozen reasons, the chief one being I have fallen in love. She makes me laugh.

  There will be an engagement ball in London—the aunts and mother insisted. You will come, of course. Invite to follow.

  Yours, with cousinly regards,

  Miles Wingate

6th Duke of Ellinbourne

P.S. I HAVE a lead on THE painting.

"Do you think he'll come?" Ann asked after she read the letter over Miles's shoulder.

"With that postscript? Yes. But I wonder if I should have written that postscript," he said.

"Why?"

He pulled her into his lap.

"It is a bit like poking the bear. What about your cousin, you really think she has the painting?"

"I questioned grandmother, and I thought about it a great deal. It is the only thing that makes sense. The painting mesmerized Helena."

"Will she recognize him?"

"How could she not! But if your cousin is that hostile to the painting, might he also be hostile to its owner?"

"He could feel that way; however, my cousin will keep that beneath the surface." He gave her light kisses on her cheek. "As someone well versed in the ways of the ton, he will not cause a scene," he said, his hands roving over her. However, it will be interesting to see how he handles it." He nuzzled her neck.

Ann arched at the feelings his lips and hands aroused in her. They took her breath away.

"Miles! We are not wed yet!" she protested weakly.

"Near enough, my love," he murmured into the side of her neck. "Near enough."

"Oh!"

The End

DON'T MISS...

AN ARTFUL COMPROMISE

Helena Littledean has a secret, a most scandalous painting she bought in discretion and keeps hidden from prying eyes. She's a young lady after all, and the Adam in her painting isn't hiding a thing behind his fig leaf. When she finally meets the Earl of Norwalk, her heart catches in her throat. It's her Adam—the embodiment of her closely held dreams standing before her...

Adam Waterbury, the Earl of Norwalk, has been trying to find Adam in the Garden of Eden for over twelve years. The artist, his maternal uncle, promised he'd never sell it, not to Adam or to anyone else. It was his masterpiece, after all. But ultimately, he sold it.

A murder visits Helena's family home, forcing her family to leave, but not before she's etched onto Adam's every waking thought. Now they are both haunted by images of the other. And then he discovered it is she who owns THE painting.

Now the question is, can Adam destroy the painting without losing Helena? If he helps solve the murder and save the Littledean business, could they come to An Artful Compromise?

252   *Don't miss…*

From your eBook
click here to get your copy

DON'T MISS...

AN ARTFUL LIE

Three years ago, Bella and Aidan were in love.

But Bella proved too valuable to the war office, her talent for cryptography unmatched, so through lies and manipulation, war office agents destroyed Bella's and Aidan's belief in each other. Emotionally ripped apart, love turned to hate.

After the war, Bella receives documents that reveal the truth. They were pawns, their love a casualty of war!

Now, could they start anew?

Jaded by war, Bella feels second chances are fairy tales. Besides, the spymaster is pressuring her to resume cryptography for a new secret service. She loves Aidan, but....

The more time Aidan spends around Bella, the more he knows he loves this woman far more than the young girl he courted three years ago. But with Bella denying them a second chance, the least he can do is see she doesn't get pressured back into spy work.

Then he discovers a specter from Bella's war past is stalking her and he'll do whatever it takes to protect her.

Don't miss…

But will it be enough?
And will he be enough for her?

From your eBook
click here to get your copy

From your eBook
click here to get your copy

CONNECTIONS

My characters come from a "connected" world. Many know each other and appear in more than one book. Sometimes they rise to the level where they need their own story.

Here are some of the connections within *Artful Deceit*.

Lord Candelstone was first mentioned in *The Waylaid Heart* as a spymaster, a behind the scenes person. He then appeared in *Rarer Than Gold* and it was his activities within that story that "encouraged" his retirement.

Mr. Lewis Martin first appeared in *Heart of a Tiger*. He has been slowly relating to me his back story – how an obviously educated man became a well-regarded Bow Street agent. We will have to see when he makes his move for center stage.

Lady Oakley was introduced in *A Grand Gesture* and has also appeared in *Heart of a Tiger*.

The Marquis who learned woodworking in order to build his daughter a rocking horse is in *The Rocking Horse – A Christmas Regency Novella*.

SCRIBBLINGS BY HOLLY NEWMAN

Flowers and Thorns *Series*
A Grand Gesture
A Heart in Jeopardy
Heart's Companion
Honor's Players

A Chance *Inquiry series*
The Waylaid Heart
Rarer Than Gold
Heart of a Tiger

Other *works*
Gentleman's Trade
Reckless Hearts
A Lady Follows
The Rocking Horse (novella)
Perchance to Dream (short story)

Coming *Soon*
Artful Deceit

ABOUT THE AUTHOR

I decided to be a writer when I was in the fifth grade. I filled notebooks with stories—until a mean-spirited high school teacher told me I had no talent for writing. Crushed, for several years I stopped writing, but writing was an itch that wouldn't go away.

My interest in the Regency period came while in high school when I volunteered to re-shelve returned books at the community library. Every week there were Georgette Heyer novels to be shelved. I finally checked one out and became immersed in the world of the Regency.

Fast forward ten years. When attending Science Fiction Conventions, I met people who read science fiction, but also enjoyed the works of Jane Austen and Georgette Heyer, just as I did! They liked these books so much that they wore Regency costumes at the science fiction conventions. They even had Regency era dancing on the convention program. These science fiction readers and writers knew a lot about the Regency era. Intrigued, I did research on the era and quickly went from casual Regency reader to a Regency history buff. Woo-hoo!

After that, with encouragement from science fiction authors, it was just a small step to writing Regencies.

After living thirty years in the Arizona desert, I now live in Florida, seven miles from the Gulf Coast, with my husband, Ken, and our six cats.

Subscribe to my newsletter to learn about books and other writings I'm working on. You can sign up here. Or visit my website